The Morganthau Affair

The Morganthau Affair

Samuel J. Zewe

Writers Club Press
San Jose New York Lincoln Shanghai

The Morganthau Affair

Writers Club Press
an imprint of iUniverse.com, Inc.

information address:
iUniverse.com, Inc.
5220 S 16th, Ste. 200
Lincoln, NE 68512
www.iuniverse.com

ISBN: 0-595-14746-1

Printed in the United States of America

To my wife Barbara, for her endless support, wisdom and laughter, I owe you more than you know.

Preface

After a brief illness I found myself thinking about the ups and downs in my life, both the good times and the really icky ones, and so I sat down one day and began to write a journal. I was told once by a respectable source that keeping a journal is a great way to try and make sense of all the clutter and chaos tumbling around in your mind, like so many bouncing rubber balls inside a metal drum.

Well, the journal idea was great and it opened a door that allowed me to explore my thoughts and organize them better than I had ever been able to do before but, to put it mildly, it was a bore. My imagination was too busy working overtime conjuring up fantasies and wild stories to be very interested in the drivel that was, and in some respects still is, my life.

One day I realized that the very act of keeping a journal had awakened something else inside me, had in fact opened another door—a hunger to tell a story, a need to breathe life into the wild imaginations that inhabit my mind. It started with a few simple quotes and phrases and grew into poetry, much to the delight of my wife, to whom most of the poems are directed.

Then one day an idea came to me for a story. I thought about it on my drive home from work where I am currently employed as an Art Director for a Houston-based energy company. All the way home I could not seem to shake the story loose from my head. The closer I got to my house the more detailed the story became until by the time I walked through the front door I couldn't wait to climb the stairs and turn on the computer and start typing.

And so, I planted myself in front of my trusty computer screen and began to type with only the vaguest idea as to where the story was headed. It began with a couple of lines of type which grew into a page that became a chapter and several months later I sat back and realized I had actually written a book. The book languished for several more months before I picked it up again and continued to hammer out the details until in early August of 2000 I decided that the book was as finished as it was ever going to get.

Along the way I have realized a few of things, that what might at first look like chaos and clutter, may in fact be an intricate jigsaw puzzle that only needs piecing together. Secondly, that there are many, many more stories like this one buried in the nooks and crannies of my mind. And what is perhaps most enjoyable is that I'm not afraid to uncover them and see what lies there.

SJZ

Acknowledgements

Although this book is a work of fiction and any resemblance to actual events, locales, places or persons, living or dead, is entirely coincidental, there is in fact a restaurant in or near the medical center of Houston, Texas that is named The Stables Restaurant and Bar. Any resemblance to The Stables Restaurant and Bar and The Stables Eatery I mention in the book are entirely coincidental. None of the employees of the book's, The Stables Eatery are based on any past or present employees of the real Stables Restaurant and Bar.

I would however, like to invite anyone who reads this book that if they should find themselves in Houston, Texas and are looking for a great place to eat, with a wonderful down home Texas atmosphere, to stop on by and order up a Texas-size steak with all the trimmings. You just might see me there.

I would also like to thank my wife Barbara, who read time and time again one rough draft after another and who caught all of those glaring errors that otherwise would have been left for the readers. Many thanks and much love.

SJZ

Chapter 1

July 21, 2000
10:00 am
Interstate 10, East of San Antonio, Texas

Just east of San Antonio, Texas on Interstate 10 heading toward Houston, a charcoal Gray Ford Mustang passes an eighteen-wheeler like it's parked for a picnic. The tires briefly hug the breakdown lane then abruptly angle back to the center of the right lane as it flies down the highway.

The driver of the car hasn't even considered what would happen if he should pass a cop at this moment, or any moment since his nightmarish dash for freedom began.

The 2000 Mustang Zach Denton is trying desperately to keep on the road is only eight months old but already looks like it took last place in one of those demolition derbies. You know the one you can't help but hear about on the television because the advertisement's announcer is practically screaming it to you.

Zach is tired, hungry and thirsty. He has zigzagged across four states sometimes reaching speeds in the triple digits, and hasn't dared stop because he knows he's a dead man if he does.

If it had not been for the fact that his Ford Mustang can only go so far on a tank of gas Zach wouldn't have even stopped long enough to fill up, much less eat or God-forbid, sleep.

He knew that running was probably futile. One of Morganthau's men was wearing and using the chip already and could home in on his thoughts as easily as if they were making a local phone call. But Zach knew the sensing equipment's capabilities had limitations.

If he could get far enough away from them he might have a shot at escaping capture. The sensing equipment was good, he knew that much and of course he had designed the chip so he knew its capability. But he was pretty sure that there was a limit to the range that the sensing equipment could reach. But how far he could only guess. He had not been part of the team of technicians and scientists that developed the sensing equipment. His claim to fame had been the chip that processed the information and made it all possible. Not that what Morganthau was using the chip for was the reason Zach had been given to build it in the first place, but it was capable just the same.

Twice, Zach could have sworn that he had managed to elude them but just when he began to feel relieved, they had shown up and almost captured him. If it hadn't been for some quick thinking and more than a little luck they would have caught him but he had managed to slip away.

But Zach knew that his luck was running out. He was tired, filthy and hungry and he was running out of road to run on. He had managed to make it has far as Texas and was currently heading toward Houston. But then what? Where would he go from there?

Zach was not sure where he would go or just what his plans were from here on out but he knew one thing for sure, he was still alive, and he planned to keep it that way.

Chapter 2

July 21, 2000
1:30 p.m.
Near downtown Houston, in the area known as the medical center.

Her name is Jamie. Zach knows because it is proudly displayed on the tag that is pinned just over her left breast.

She has a sweet, innocent look about her. She's young, perhaps just barely in her twenties. She is a hostess at the restaurant Zachary Denton has just ducked into. The restaurant and Jamie are in stark contrast to the bleached white hot and desperately humid day he has escaped from. He would not swear by it, but Zach thought the climate in Houston was hotter by a long shot than what he left behind in Nevada, New Mexico and Arizona.

"At least in Nevada, New Mexico and Arizona you do not get the feeling that you're wearing the air like a overstuffed coat," Zach thought to himself.

As Zach entered the restaurant he ran his fingers through his hair in a vain attempt to tidy his appearance. He adjusted his shirt and hitched up his slacks that were looking droopy on his thinning frame of a body. He stepped quietly into the cool confines of the restaurant and was immediately rewarded by a blast of cold air from the air-duct placed strategically over the door. Relishing the cold air on his body Zach looked around the dark interior of the restaurant.

It is one of those chains of eating establishments that could be almost anywhere. With its dark stained wood and brass accents and the smell of meat cooking over an open grille it could pass for any one of a thousand restaurants across the US, accept the name. "The Stables Eatery," Zach turned the name over in his head.

"Maybe because I feel like crap, the name just fit my mood," he thought as his attention turned to the prettiest face he had ever seen.

Like the dark inviting allure of the restaurant, the young woman Zach now gazed upon was equally enticing. She is only slightly shorter than Zach's five feet-nine inch frame. But there, the similarities end. She is slender but not thin, with the curves and lines of an actress or model.

"She definitely could be either in my book," Zach thinks.

"Smoking or non-smoking," she asks.

Momentarily dumbfounded by her beauty, Zach says, "ah, smoking."

"Come this way, please," she replies as she reaches for a menu and turns to walk away.

Again, Zach finds himself unable to either speak or move as he watches her seductive-like retreat. "I have definitely got to come back here and ask her out, that is, if I get out of this alive," Zach thinks to himself.

Zach laughs silently to himself thinking how absurd that sounds. To think that Morganthau's men are going to just let him go after he led them on a wild-goose chase half way across the US was a real joke. Zach knows he's as good as dead if they catch him.

Snapping out of the trance he has fallen into, Zach obediently follows the hostess around the corner and to the awaiting booth, again his eyes are drawn to the clinging black lace dress that entangles her body.

"I want you bad," Zach mutters to himself unable to take his eyes from the curve of her slim seductive hips.

He must have said it louder than he thought for she turns toward Zach with a wink in her eye, and whispers, "I'm not on the menu, but maybe we could work something out."

Then in a more business-like tone she says, "your waitress will be with you in a moment, if there is anything else I can do for you please let me know." With a smile, she turns and walks away leaving Zach red faced and quite embarrassed. She turns back once, Zach guessed to see just how many shades of red he had become.

*   *   *

Zach did not have to ask her for a booth in the back for she has seated him where both the entrance (as well as the hostess station where she now stands) and the emergency exit are all quite visible. He gives himself a mental slap across the face to jolt him out of the trance he has slipped into since he gazed upon her beautiful body and stared into those eyes that are the color of jade.

"I would have to stand in a pretty long line to get a chance with someone as drop dead gorgeous as her," Zach thought.

He breaks free of the trance and scans the restaurant to see if anyone is looking in his general direction and at the same time looks out the windows that surround the restaurant to the parking lot and street beyond.

"It looks safe enough, for now," Zach thinks to himself.

He asked to be seated in the smoking section not because he smokes, he hates cigarette smoke, it makes his eyes water, but to be away from other people just in case something should happen while he's here. Just in case they find him.

When he first pulled into the parking lot he had looked around to see how many cars were parked by the restaurant and had decided that there were few enough that he could chance stopping and getting something to eat.

He must have timed it right between the lunch and dinner crowds because as he walked in he could see that there were only two tables currently occupied with patrons.

Two women occupied one table, Zach judged each to be about forty years old, laughing and talking up a storm. Zach could hear one woman telling the other something about finding her boss in a compromising position with a co-worker and exactly at what moment she had made this mind-blowing discovery.

The other table was further down the aisle from the two bantering women and was filled to the brim with teenagers who were engrossed in their own conversation and were too far away for Zach to catch anything they were saying.

A rather bland looking waitress hurled herself down the aisle toward the table where Zach sat. Pulling out a large white pad from the green apron that was tied around her waist to take his order, she said, "Hi, My name is Fran. I'll be your waitress today."

"Nice to meet you Fran," Zach said absently as his gaze went to the tee shirt the waitress wore. It displayed the restaurant logo at the top and below the logo it read, 'Steaks as big as Texas!' in big bold print.

"Can I get you something to drink?" she beams. Her voice taking on a high pitched whine not unlike that of a DC-10's jet engines as it would sound as it began its slow lumbering takeoff.

"Something cold, with lots of ice, a coke, better yet, make it a rum and coke," Zach tells her.

"You got it," she announces more to the entire restaurant than to him. "Anything else," she blared.

"A cheeseburger and fries," Zach says not bothering to look at the menu for fear he would have to endure more of the waitress' trumpeting voice.

"Okey dokey," she cheerfully yells to the rest of the tables as she turns and races off.

"It's a good thing this place is relatively empty," he thinks, as he reaches down and retracts the Smith and Wesson 9mm from the inside of his right boot and places it under the napkin now covering his lap.

"Just in case," Zach says to himself, looking again to the windows, and life's goings-on beyond them.

Zach never liked guns. In fact he loathed them. But this was different. Someone was chasing him and he knew if they caught up to him he'd probably wind up dead. So he had decided to stop and buy a gun on his wild dash for freedom and had picked up this piece from a pawnshop. The guy behind the counter didn't ask questions and gladly took Zach's MasterCard. Without so much as a questioning look the store clerk had dropped the gun and the ammunition into a brown paper bag like it was a candy bar and a soft drink he had just purchased instead of a lethal weapon and away Zach went.

"Hell, I have never even fired a gun before. I'm not sure I know how," he thought.

The waitress breezed by depositing his drink on the table without missing a beat saying, "Here you go," fifty decibels too loud, and continued on in a rush as if the place was packed to the rafters, which it is not. It takes less than ten minutes for Fran to return with Zach's food. She retrieves his now empty glass and asks if he would like another.

Zach replies, "Could you make that a glass of water with lemon, one drink is enough for me."

"Sure thing, Hon," she says and bounces off stopping briefly at one empty table after another as if people were actually sitting there waiting for her to take their order.

"Man, am I starving," Zach thinks to himself as he tears into the burger, shoving a handful of fries in after it for good measure. He has to stifle a laugh when the thought of choking to death on food pops into his mind.

"After all I have just been through, choking to death on a burger would be a breeze compared to what those goons will do to me if they catch me," he thinks. It's then that he realizes it has been three days since he has eaten, three days since…

"Sir? Hey, Mister? Are you all right?"

Fran is shouting at him Zach realizes. He must have looked to her like he really was choking with a mouthful of food and a blank look on his face.

"Here's your water, Are you sure your OK?" she asks in that megaphone voice of hers.

"Ah, yes, yes, just lost in thought for a moment." "Maybe a little tired, too," he added more to himself.

With a questioning look upon her face she sets the glass of water on the table and turns and leaves and just as quickly as she appeared she is gone again.

Zach resumes devouring the burger and fries, marveling at how wonderful it taste and thinking whether or not he will ever be able to enjoy another meal like this again. Three days he's been on the run without stopping to eat or sleep, three days since the Morganthau affair began.

Chapter 3

July 21, 2000
1:15 p.m.
The Stables Eatery, Houston, Texas

Jamie heard the car before she ever saw it pull into the parking lot. Driving past the entrance to the restaurant now and just as quickly vanishing around the corner to come to a screeching halt in a parking space by the side of the building. The person behind the wheel sat in the car for a moment looking around the parking lot as if expecting to see someone else pull up beside him.

"Probably a lovers rendezvous," she surmised, and half-thinking to herself she wondered what it would be like to make it with a married man.

"What am I saying," she thought, "I've never been with a man, much less a married one." Laughing, and somewhat surprised by her own lustful wondering, she turned her attention back to folding the napkins in that decorative fan-like pattern she had been taught when she first started at "The Stables Eatery".

"The Stables Eatery" was a family owned and operated eating establishment located in the heart of the medical center, in the over crowded and much too international for her taste, city of Houston, Texas. It was not that she disliked foreigners or crowds for that matter. It was just that she wasn't use to so many diverse cultures. Having spent the first eighteen years of her life growing up on a farm in Alvin, Texas, some thirty miles to the south of Houston, it might as well have been three thousand miles away for all the traveling she got to do. The only time she ever left her hometown was when she got to go on the FFA sponsored trips to other schools in the equally small towns around Alvin.

"I am not about to spend the rest of my life as some back woods country farm girl," she remembered telling her dad one day during a heated argument years ago. Adding insult to injury she also remembers saying that the last thing she was going to do was shovel crap in her father's horse stables or any stable for that matter ever again.

Well, here she was, a twenty year old country girl living in a big city, waiting tables at a place called "The Stables Eatery", cleaning up after and getting pawed nightly by the animals who arrogantly referred to themselves as the elite social class of Houston. If her dad were alive, she thought with a tear in her eye, he'd probably think it a real hoot. She missed her dad. She missed him a lot.

She missed having a father figure in her life. Someone you could rely on to be there when things seemed to be at their worst. It had been five years now since her father's death and life on the farm just hadn't been the same. He had died on his way home from work on a hot July night after staying too late at the downtown office building where he worked, having one too many drinks with the co-owners in his oil tool supply business.

She remembered, as if it were yesterday, saying good-bye to him that morning as he left for work. Bending down to plant a kiss on her forehead, "see you later, small fry," he had said. And then he was gone from her life forever.

"Five years to the day and ten days before my fifteenth birthday", she thought.

"Life sucks," she mumbled to herself.

Jamie started thinking about the nickname her dad had given her so long ago. He had always called her "small fry," he had told her once, ever since the day she arrived into the world kicking and screaming. Her dad said that when she was born her mother ask her father what they were going to name the baby and he said with a grin, how about "Small," since their last name was Fry. But her mother just looked at him with the tired eyes of someone who had just been through a long and painful ordeal so he said, "all right, how about Jamie after your mother," since he knew that's what her mother had wanted to call her all along.

Jamie had been her grandmother's name, the grandmother she could only see in the photographs that had been taken of her shortly before she had died of cancer, just two short months before Jamie had been born. She remembered how her grandmother looked in the photos and thinking how she reminded her of the ex-First Lady of the United States, Barbara Bush.

"A nice lady," she thought.

Jamie remembered the countless times she would hold a tea party for her dolls and how she would pretend to invite her grandmother to them. She would ask her how she was doing and what were heaven like and all the other questions little girls ask. She had always felt like she had missed out on something special by not ever having met her grandmother.

Jamie was lost in thought and unaware that someone had walked into the restaurant. She looked up with a start to see a man staring back at her. Well, not exactly at her, more at her breasts, she guessed from the way his mouth hung open.

Mama used to tell me she thought, "Jamie, you stand there slack-jawed much longer a family of flies are gonna have a picnic in your mouth." Mama was such a redneck.

"Smoking or non-smoking," she asked the man. It takes him several seconds to respond, she notices with some pleasure. Smiling more to her self than to the gawking, but rather nice looking man; she turns, grabs a menu and motions for him to follow.

"I can just image what he's looking at now," she thinks, still smiling to herself as she ushers him to a booth around the corner. Jamie knew what most men had on their minds. It was rare that she would find a man who actually talked to her instead of at her breasts.

"What has gotten into me," she wonders as she feels her face become flush. She returns to her hostess station thinking, "Well, I'm sure he did not mean for me to hear, but I can't believe I responded to him like that." "I have definitely got to get a boyfriend," she says to herself. "Being a virgin is the pits."

She promised her dad right after she hit the ripe old age of thirteen that she wasn't going to have anything to do with boys ever. Troy Brackson, the star pitcher for the Alvin Tiger's baseball team, had knocked up her best friend Jessie, on the night of their big win against the Texas City Stingrays.

Jessie was only fourteen at the time and scared out of her wits. She waited almost a month before she told Jamie, her best friend no less, that her period was late, and then when she began to show, she went and tried to perform an abortion on herself.

Jamie never got to speak to Jessie again because right after it happened Jessie went to live with her Aunt and Uncle up in Dallas. Jamie's dad sat her down a few days later and told her that Jessie came within seconds of dying. You could always tell when dad was being serious. It was the only time he would use her real name. He said, "Jamie, you know that you can come to me anytime, for anything, no matter what the problem, even if it was from something as serious as getting pregnant."

But he laid the guilt on heavy then by including that it would just about break his heart to find out that his little girl had begun having sexual intercourse. From then on whenever Jamie went out with a boy he was apt to get a punch in the eye as kissed, and after her dad died she couldn't seem to get her promise to him out of her head. By then all the boys in town had learned to stay well away from her.

"So much for dating life in a small town," she thought miserably.

"Life may have sucked back on the farm but things are looking up," she thought as she found herself glancing over her shoulder at the rugged looking man in the booth whose attention was temporarily focused on devouring the meal he had ordered.

"And from the looks of it, if he makes love like he consumes food I would be in for the ride of my life," she breathed out.

Feeling thoroughly flushed now, she tried to turn away and focus her attention on folding napkins. Try as she might to ignore the man in the booth her eyes were continually drawn to that side of the restaurant in hopes of getting a better look at his face. He was perhaps in his mid-thirties and a few inches taller than she was, with a stunning pair of blue eyes. With the exception of a few days growth of beard he was well groomed with brownish-blond hair kept fairly short, like he had just had it cut recently. He did not appear to be overly muscular but neither was he overweight.

"I'd definitely let him eat crackers in my bed," she thought, blushing again. That he appeared slightly nervous and a little tired, made her wonder if maybe he could be in some kind of trouble.

"Hmm, an older man, on the run from the law meets young beautiful woman," "news at Eleven," Jamie jokingly thought. Ever since her father died she found herself more and more attracted to older men. The school psychologist said that it was natural to look for a replacement father figure after the death of her dad.

"But I do not think she meant it in quite this way," Jamie thought.

Chapter 4

July 21, 2000
1:45 p.m.
The Stables Restaurant, Houston, Texas

Zach was only mildly distracted by the waitresses' comings and goings and his own hunger that was beginning to subside, thanks to the burger and fries he had just consumed in record speed. Ever since he had managed to escape from the "compound", as Morganthau liked to call it, he was constantly on the alert for any signs that Morganthau's men had picked up his trail again.

Morganthau was the president of Technadine Corporation where Zach had hired on just eight months ago in their microchip design division. At sixty-one, Morganthau was an imposing figure of a man. He stood six feet four inches tall and checked in at two hundred fifty pounds. But it wasn't just his size that won him the most-feared man-of-the-year award. He was one of the most wealthy and powerful men in the valley due largely to his dealings with the military and US Government. He worked closely with presidential advisors and military officials in some of the most top-secret projects the Government has ever conjured up. They trusted him with secrets that even Presidents did not have access. When Morganthau wanted something he usually got it, and so it was not hard for him to go looking for Zach Denton when word got around of Zach's achievements in microchip design at a local company.

Morganthau easily lured Zach away from his job at a small computer gaming firm in Silicon Valley to the high tech labs that took up half of Technadine's main headquarters covering some twenty-acre's of prime real estate. With it's tight security and modern but imposing structure, the Technadine labs stood out among the other office buildings that made up the roughly twelve square miles of Silicon Valley.

While most of the companies in the valley were happily designing hardware and software for computer games and non-lethal forms of entertainment, Technadine was quietly pushing out super sophisticated surveillance and detection equipment for the military and other branches of the US Government.

Soon after arriving at Technadine's labs Zach became suspicious of Morganthau and his reasons for bringing Zach on board. Zach had begun to suspect Morganthau was using him and when he began going through the companies secret personnel records and Morganthau's own personal memo's, Zach knew he was in over his head.

He had learned Morganthau's top securities man Joseph Whiteslayer, whose personnel file read like America's most wanted, was a natural born hunter and tracker with a penchant for killing. He came from a long line of Cheyenne warriors who terrorized the white settlers as they moved west across the central plains during the 1800's. Whiteslayer had been in and out of trouble both on and off the reservation since he was old enough to walk.

At just seventeen, Whiteslayer had been shipped off to the army by the counsel of elders of the Indian reservation where he lived, because they feared him so. Trouble followed him in the Army and it was only after he was assigned to Morganthau's command that things began to look up for Whiteslayer.

Zach was sure that Whiteslayer was one of the men now hunting him and equally aware of just what they intended to do to him once they caught him and had managed to torture the last remaining codes from his mind. Zach knew that they would indeed get all the information they wanted and with sadistic pleasure. These were not your normal nine to five businessmen that had been hunting him across four states like he was some small scared creature in a cross-country foxhunt.

They had all been a part of a highly trained and extremely secretive platoon of the Special Forces division of the U.S. Army. Whiteslayer had been the youngest of them all and had also proved to be the meanest. Morganthau took an instant liking to Whiteslayer and the two became inseparable. Morganthau had been their commanding officer and the team quickly made a name for themselves as being the most feared and ruthless the army had ever seen.

The army also saw in them and their commander a chance to try out some top-secret test on the team, experiments not even the President of the United States knew about. The military had long been studying the plausibility of ESP, (Extra-Sensory Perception) under combat conditions and had decided to make Morganthau's outfit the subject for new and even more sinister applications of this phenomenon.

Army scientists had been studying the effects of certain drugs on the sensory preceptors of the brain in hopes of concocting an ESP inducer that would trigger certain auditory and neuro-transmitters to heighten these areas and give the men the ability to hear each others thoughts. They also hoped the drugs would give the men the ability to hear others not in the test group, making them especially useful for espionage work abroad.

"These were not nice guys," Zach thought as he played back in his mind all the details he had uncovered in those documents at Technadine.

"It was scary to think what the US Government had it's hands in, and the people of the United States knew nothing about its secret dealings. People go about their day-to-day lives sometimes totally oblivious of what atrocities their own government deals in", he thought.

"It is enough to make you curl up in a corner and cover your head," Zach thought as he glanced over at the two ladies chatting away on the other side of the restaurant.

As Zach was looking across the restaurant and thinking what a mess he had gotten into, a white unmarked van pulled into the parking lot, rounding the corner of the restaurant and disappeared around the back to where the service entrance was located. Four large men climbed nonchalantly from the side door of the van looking very much like ordinary businessmen out for a late power lunch except for the weapons each was holding in their hands.

Two of the men went immediately to the service entrance door, while the other two men each took up a position at the back two corners of the restaurant. The leader of the four men, Joseph Whiteslayer, tried the door and giving a nod with his head to indicate that the door was unlocked, proceeded to open the door and enter. Just as quickly the big man standing by the door next to Whiteslayer disappeared through the opening.

*   *   *

Known by his buddies as "The Duke," because of the John Wayne-like swagger in his walk that he developed after having a land mine go off five feet from where he and another platoon buddy had been standing. The blast had lifted Duke and the other soldier off their feet and thrown them thirty feet in the air before landing again in the rice field they had been walking through. Some shrapnel in his hip was the extent of Duke's injuries; however, his buddy did not fair so well, the blast tearing him in half before it reached Duke.

Duke didn't mind the shrapnel near as much as the venereal disease he had gotten from that oriental bitch while recuperating from his injuries in Saigon. She had been a small slender girl of about eighteen and could fuck like a pro, which was exactly what she probably had been, but Duke hadn't asked and they had spent several days together drinking and fucking like rabbits.

Then he had started to itch and his pecker began to sting every time he had to pee and before long the pain in his crotch even over-shadowed the pain in his hip. Duke was sure his pecker was going to rot off before he had finally gone to the doc and gotten some medication for the infection.

Duke and his older brother Chad had both enlisted in the Marines in '71, within months of each other. Duke was just finishing up boot camp when Chad's platoon headed 'in-country' for the first time. Their mother was distraught over the decision of her "baby boys" to join the service after she had made it clear throughout their young lives that they weren't going to share the same fate as their dad who had been killed in Korea in '54. Both boys had grown up fascinated with war and had secretly shared in looking at their father's old military photos, which they carefully hid from their mom. The boys had found them one day in the attic and from that day forward had each made a vow to one day join the Marines.

Dukes' brother had been killed just three months after his platoon had landed in Vietnam. In fact, the whole platoon had been wiped out in a matter of minutes after coming on some V.C. in a small village outside of Tran Nang. They were cut down so fast that only a couple of them had had time to even leap for cover. His brother Chad had been one of the unlucky ones to survive the initial onslaught. Wounded and bleeding badly he had managed to pull himself to a small ditch where he returned fire until his ammunition ran out. The V.C. waited until they were sure he could no longer return fire and casually walked up to him and took turns hacking him to death.

After his Mom received word of her oldest son's death she took to drinking and never let up until the day they found her dead and cold lying in her own vomit on the floor of her bedroom. Duke got the letter from home two weeks after hearing that his older brother had also been killed. Now, it seemed to Duke that he was carrying the weight of his whole family on his shoulders.

But he loved the military and had no plans of backing down now. He loved the smell of Napalm in the morning. He loved the closeness of his platoon buddies and the adrenaline rush he got when they made a successful raid on a village. He was definitely at his happiest when he was in the military.

Having been through as much as Duke had been through in his young life most kids would probably shy away from such things as war and booze. But a long time ago Duke and his brother had sat up in that dark musty-smelling attic and each made a promise that they would take up where their father had left off. They wanted to be Marines and everything that came with it.

Duke was military all the way, at forty-seven years-old and still sporting a crew cut and looking as fit as the day he came out of boot camp.

Right about now though Duke was wondering how he went from being a respected ex-Marine to being in the company of this psycho, Whiteslayer, and why he was chasing some little punk of a man across four states. He was just thinking he could use a stiff drink when the psycho nudged him in the ribs.

*   *   *

Duke and Whiteslayer were in a small alcove in the storage area of the restaurant, just behind the kitchen where two young men and a woman were busily preparing for the dinner crowd that would begin milling into the place in another couple of hours. Whiteslayer and Duke moved from the protection of the alcove and proceeded around the corner and into the kitchen where the three employees were working.

As fast as lightning, Whiteslayer walked up to the biggest of the two workers and dropped him with a backhand to the base of the neck. The woman and the other male cook were so stunned they just stood there with their mouths open unable to speak. Whiteslayer pushed the Glock 9mm under the chin of the second man and said, "make a sound and I will blow your fucking head off."

The cook realizing he was still holding the ten-inch carving knife and acting on dumb blind instinct swung the knife at the man with the gun. Whiteslayer saw the man react and with a smile of satisfaction on his face shot out his own hand cupping the cook's hand in his and turning the angle of the blade, drove it to the hilt into the cooks rib cage. The woman screamed as the cook let out a dying gasp and fell to the floor. Whiteslayer shot out his other hand, like a snake striking it's victim and hit her with the butt of the pistol, silencing the scream.

*   *   *

Jake, the oldest of the Technadine security team and his partner, Taz, had moved around to the front two corners of the building, each positioning themselves to stop anyone from escaping through the front entrance. Jake moved in as close to the doors as possible. He tried to stay as low to the ground as a six-foot tall three hundred-pound person of his age could get. Jake knew he was too fat and way too old for this kind of shit but it's all he had ever known, having fought as a mercenary in more countries and way too many wars than he cared to remember. He got to within eight feet of the door and sat low with his back to the building and waited. He got himself settled and then peered around the corner to see if Taz was in place.

Taz, by far the most maniacal of the four, stayed by the far corner of the building opposite where Jake was stationed and in plain site of the van. In case Zach did manage to get past the others, he could still get to the van and run him down if it came to it. Taz was probably the least liked of the team because his spastic, jittery demeanor and constant mumbling, Jake thought it made him look like one of those street people you see occasionally standing on the corner talking to themselves, hands gesturing to no one in particular. He made Jake and the others nervous, especially since he was their driver.

As long as they kept him in a Prozac induced haze he was perfectly fine and you wouldn't know anything was wrong. But a few times he had decided that he did not need his medication any longer and they found themselves racing down some freeway at a hundred plus miles-per-hour changing lanes faster than you could blink. Taz would start singing children's songs at the top of his lungs and steering the van from one lane to another without looking first to see if any other cars were on the road. "Nervous was not the word for it," Jake thought.

       *   *   *

Zach was jolted out of thought by the sound of a scream cut painfully short. It had originated from the back of the restaurant and just as quickly as it started it had stopped. Zach looked around quickly at the other patrons of the restaurant to see if they too had heard the scream. The restaurant had grown eerily quiet with all eyes turned in the direction the scream had originated.

He leaped to his feet, grabbing the gun from his lap and jacking a round in the chamber, Zach ran to the front of the restaurant where the hostess was now looking towards the kitchen to see what all the commotion was.

A man appeared from the kitchen area, wearing a business suit and sporting a military style hair cut, looked in Zach's direction and said, "didn't think we would find you, did you?" Just as he spoke, Fran, Zach's waitress, came screaming around the corner wanting to know what all the fuss was about and was shot once through the throat.

"Shut up bitch," Duke said as he pulled the trigger sending Fran flying backward over a table with blood spewing from what was left of her neck and her dying body crashing to the floor in a heap.

Fran's body came to a rest in a sitting position with her back pressed against the edge of a booth, head lolling to one side, eyes fixed on a salt shaker that had fallen to the floor. Her chest heaved in a futile attempt to suck in one last breath of air but without most of her windpipe intact to guide the air to her aching lungs, all that was managed was this awful retching-hitching sound as blood gurgled out of the gaping wound.

Almost simultaneously the two women in the front of the restaurant let out blood curdling screams, but quickly covered their mouths with shocked horror as Duke swung his pistol in their direction intending to shoot them both if they continued to scream for even a second longer.

That was all the time Zach needed. He had reacted too late to stop the man from shooting Fran but raised his own pistol and fired twice at Duke, shattering the big man's knee with the first shot and striking him in the shoulder just above the heart with the second. The man stumbled over a chair, lost his footing and crashed to the ground, dropping his gun as he went down in agonizing pain. The gun slid across the floor and came to a rest under one of the booths by the window.

Jamie was screaming as Zach grabbed her and started to pull her toward the door, "run!" he shouted at her.

She turned and fled through the door not even looking back for fear she would be killed if she did. She made it to the walkway just outside the door when someone hiding just out of view grabbed her. Jake reached out and grabbed her by the hair with his left hand yanking her backward and then sinking the claws of his big meaty right hand around her mouth to stifle a scream that had formed in Jamie's throat.

With all her strength Jamie shot out an elbow and connected with the big man's stomach that had become soft with old age. Jake let out a rush of air as he released her, trying to catch his breath. Before he could take another breath Jamie turned and kick as hard as she could into the big man's groin sending him to the ground where he lay in a fetal position coughing and gasping for air.

Without knowing why she reached down and picked up the gun that had dropped from the mans hand and then ran as fast as she could to the safety of her car that was parked five rows away from the front of the restaurant's entrance.

Still clutching her purse, Jamie fumbled for the keys. A moment earlier she had been about to re-apply some lipstick when all the excitement had begun and fled with purse in hand when Zach shoved her toward the door. Finding the keys she shoved them into the door lock and then jumped into the car. Only then did she manage to turn and look at the entrance to the restaurant to see what was happening.

Zach was backing towards the door when Whiteslayer came around the corner from the kitchen, his gun pointed down by his side and said, "Zach, you know you can not hide."

"There is no place you can run to that I can not find you. Come with me and I promise you will not get hurt" Whiteslayer said.

"Fuck you, asshole," Zach replied as he raised the pistol in his hands and began spraying bullets in Whiteslayer's direction.

Whiteslayer dove for cover not wanting to give the guy a lucky shot. He hoped Zach would run out of ammo so he could finish this mess and get this sorry little shit back to the compound. Morganthau wanted him alive at all cost and it had already cost him one man as Whiteslayer could see by the looks of his buddy lying on the floor six feet away.

"Come on Zach, give us the codes to the chips and we will let you go, I promise," Whiteslayer said, knowing the second he had those codes he'd cut off Zach's nuts and feed them to him one by one.

"The sorry shit," he thought. But he never got a reply for as he looked around the corner Zach had already exited the building.

"Shit," he yelled.

Before he'd taken six steps toward the door he saw that Taz had jumped in the van they had rented and come flying around the corner headed straight for Zach who had stopped running and was staring back towards the restaurant. Whiteslayer then watched helplessly as Zach raised his pistol and fired at the van sending it careening out of control to slam into a parked truck. His anger swelled within him as he saw Zach run to a waiting car, jump in and then watched as they sped off.

"The girl from the restaurant," he thought.

"Damn, they let him get away," Whiteslayer screamed, then turned and glared at the frightened patrons of the restaurant who had all scurried for cover under tables and chairs, like scared little rabbits, when the shooting started.

One of the ladies was blubbering like a lost child in a department store so Whiteslayer calmly walked over to her and as he shot her three times in the head he said, "shut up, bitch!" a bullet striking her body with each word he spoke.

He could not think with all that noise in the background. Whiteslayer turned and walked over to the other man who had been his backup when he entered the restaurant. The man was breathing but he was in serious shape with a bullet wound just over his heart that had no doubt hit an artery judging from the amount of blood that had pooled around him.

"Zach may be just a nerdy little computer 'techie' but he can still shoot a gun," he thought as he looked down at his fallen buddy. He knew he did not have time to help him and he could not leave him here and risk having him talk, so he calmly placed his revolver one foot from the man's turned head and pulled the trigger. With a loud bang that echoed through the restaurant, the body jerked once and was still.

"Sorry pal, but I had to do it," Whiteslayer said with very little emotion in his voice. He went through his dead buddy's pockets and took all of the credentials making sure there were no links to Technadine and then walked outside into the hot afternoon sunshine.

"Why would anyone want to live here, it feels like the jungles back in Nam," he thought as his shirt under his suit coat had already begun to stick to him from the humidity that hung in the air like sheets of invisible rain.

*   *   *

Zach half ran, half dove for the front entrance to the restaurant not sure what he would do when he reached the parking lot but knowing that if he stayed he was a goner. He almost tripped over the man lying on the sidewalk as he ran toward the street, only briefly connecting the man with the familiar face at Technadine as that of the big teddy bear of a man named Jake. The man was reaching for him but it was obvious he was in no condition to stop Zach or anyone else for that matter. Zach did not know what had happened to him and did not care. He just wanted to get away, as far away as possible.

Zach turned and ran into the parking lot trying to put as much distance between him and Morganthau's men as he could. He had gone only a short distance when he heard the sound of a car behind him and to his right racing through the parking lot. He stopped and turned just as a white van tore around the corner of the building heading straight for him as if the person behind the wheel intended to run him down.

Zach hesitated, trying to decide if he could out run the approaching van. Seeing that the parking lot was relatively empty and there was no place that could prevent him from being crushed under the weight of the fast moving vehicle, he stopped and turned toward the approaching van. He took a deep breath, raised his pistol and fired two times into the windshield on the driver's side of the speeding van. A large spider's web appeared to form out of nowhere as the first bullet struck the windshield just to the right and high of the driver's side of the van.

The second round must have hit its mark as he watched the windshield explode inward and saw the driver of the van thrown back, hard against the seat, then slump forward over the steering wheel. The van veered sharply to the left and plowed into a parked pickup truck with a KIKK country radio station sticker on the back window.

"That's going to be one ticked off country boy," Zach thought.

He turned and started to run toward some stores on the other side of the small strip center he was in when he caught a glimpse of a face staring back at him through the side window of a yellow Ford Mustang. It was the girl from the restaurant.

         *   *   *

Jamie looked at the man standing by her car and then looked in the direction of the restaurant and the man she had kneed in the crotch seconds earlier. He was standing now, holding himself and looking at the man who was standing next to her car and looking at her. It was one of those eerie sort of moments when no one knows quite what to do next, but in an instant she made up her mind and rolled down her window and yelled for the obviously frightened man to climb in.

Zach at first shook his head, waving her off, but after taking another look behind him at the restaurant he decided he had little choice and ran around to the passenger side of the car and climbed in.

Jamie took off like a shot, tearing out of the parking lot and into the street pushing the car to seventy before she had gone a block. She drove for five minutes constantly looking in all the mirrors and turning her head to see if anyone was following them before she ever said a word to Zach.

"This may sound like a really bad time to be asking this," she said, "but what the hell was that all about?" she screamed at Zach, her voice rising with each word that came out.

Zach looked into those beautiful but extremely frightened eyes of hers and putting out his right hand in a gesture of introductions, said, "my name is Zachary Denton and I want to thank you for saving my life," he said.

Jamie took hold of his hand noticing the slight trembling of his handshake and also that he was a nail biter. "He must be one of those personalities with a lot of pent-up energy. Always looking for something to do, can't-stop-moving-types," Jamie thought.

"I'm not sure it's a pleasure meeting you, but hello anyway," she said.

"Can you please tell me what just happened and who those men were back there?"

"Maybe I'd better start at the beginning," Zach said. "By the way, nice choice of car you got here," running his hand over the smooth black leather interior and thinking of his own Mustang back at the restaurant.

"My name, as I've already told you, is Zach Denton. I am thirty-two years-old and I was born in Canton Ohio, but I've been living and working in Silicon Valley since I graduated from Stanford University almost ten years ago. It's the same school where the title of "Father of Silicon Valley," belongs to the brilliant Stanford University professor of electrical engineering, Frederick Terman. In a way he was my mentor.

Anyway, I worked for some small time companies around Silicon Valley before being hired on at a corporation called Technadine where they make super sophisticated electronic detection and surveillance equipment. I worked in their microchip design division, hell, I became their microchip division," he said, showing little modesty.

"The guys that Morganthau had hired before me couldn't design their way out of a paper bag."

Somewhat embarrassed by his own cockiness he continued, "anyway, I was working on my life long dream to create the first true artificially intelligent microprocessor. I thought it was going to be used for many things that I considered good for mankind, but after I had completed one of the processors Morganthau shut me out of the next phase of the project, hell, he cast me off like I was a nobody. So I started to do some checking through the computer files and I found these."

Zach reached into his shirt pocket and withdrew some folded pieces of computer paper and handed them to Jamie.

Chapter 5

July 21, 2000

1:55 p.m.

The Stables Restaurant, Houston, Texas

Jake had finally gotten to his feet and holding his still aching crotch, went to check on his buddy, Taz, in the van. Finding him dead he emptied his pockets and then pulled the body from behind the wheel as if he were nothing more than a sack of garbage to be left by the curb.

"Dumb ass crazy fool," he said to the corpse. He climbed into the van after checking the damage and being satisfied that it was still in driveable condition, backed it away from the truck it had plowed into and drove to the front of the restaurant where Whiteslayer was now standing. Whiteslayer jumped into the passenger seat of the van and ordered Jake to drive around to the side of the restaurant and had him stop next to Zach's car.

Whiteslayer got out and looked in through the window of the car to see if he could spot the documents Zach had taken from the compound. Not seeing them in the car he went around the back of the car to the trunk and pulled a set of tools from his pocket and began working on the lock to the trunk trying to force it open. With the sound of sirens growing louder in the distance he quickly jimmied the lock and popped the trunk open to reveal a box full of documents covered by a towel. He tossed aside the towel and grabbed the box and leaving the trunk wide open walked back to the van and climbed inside. They drove off just as the first of what was to be several police cars pulled into the parking lot.

"Without these documents Zach can not do much harm now but we still need to find him and fast," Whiteslayer said.

Whiteslayer directed his man to drive in the direction he had sensed Zach was going and then sat back in the seat to concentrate, trying to pick up Zach's thoughts. With an intense look of concentration washing over and altering his otherwise stoic facial features, he focused in to see where Zach was headed next. Just maybe, if he could lock on long enough to Zach's thoughts, he would get the information he needed.

Ten minutes went by then twenty, and then with a smile he relaxed and turned to his surviving partner and said, "they're headed to Dallas. Take the I-45 North Freeway, it will take us right to him."

Chapter 6

July 21, 2000
2:15 p.m.
Technadine Corporation, Silicon Valley, California

On the third ring, Douglas J. Morganthau picked up the phone in his plush office on the top floor of the International offices of Technadine Corporation. He was hoping for good news. It was not.

"What do you mean he got away?" he said into the receiver, his voice quickly taking on a strained sound.

Whiteslayer explained to him what had happened, leaving out the messy details in the restaurant, but before he could tell him about the two men that were killed he was cut off, "I want him back here in twenty-four hours."

"Is that clear?" Morganthau screamed.

"Affirmative," Whiteslayer started to say but was cut off as Morganthau slammed down the receiver.

"Damn!" Morganthau yelled to his empty office.

Chapter 7

As they sped through Houston Zach decided to continue driving north to Dallas where they would look for a non-descriptive motel to stay the night in. From there Zach did not know what they would do or where they would go, so long as Morganthau's men were after him he supposed he would just keep running forever.

After they had headed out of Houston on Interstate 45 North towards Dallas, Zach had Jamie pull into one of those combination gas station/grocery stores in the town of Conroe. Jamie's car was running on fumes so he told her to pull into the Shamrock station just off the feeder road of I-45. Zach also wanted to pick up some bandages and Peroxide to cleanse the cuts on Jamie's face that she had received while fighting off the big man in front of the restaurant.

While Zach went into the store, Jamie sat in the car and read the documents that Zach had handed her has they raced out of Houston. She did not understand much of the technical jargon written in the documents, but she did grasp the underlying tone, and it scared her.

She knew there were sick, greedy people like this Morganthau guy in the world but she was shocked at how her own Government could back someone so deviant and self-serving. It became obvious to her; the more she read that this Morganthau character wanted nothing less than total, world domination.

She then had a thought, "maybe the Government does know what he is up to and is letting him do all the dirty work for them only to get rid of him after the plan is in place."

The thought made her shudder as if a cold arctic wind had just entered the car, even though the temperature outside was reaching a blistering one hundred degrees.

Chapter 8

July 21, 2000
2:40 p.m.
Technadine Corporation, Silicon Valley, California

Morganthau sat in his office behind his imported teakwood desk with cherry accents grinding a pencil into its smooth glossy finish.

"If they screw this up I will kill them all with my own two hands," he fumed.

Morganthau was accustomed to having things go his way and this little problem with Denton was getting way out of hand. He knew he shouldn't have put so much trust in one designer. He should have instituted more checks and balances, more back-up provisions from the start.

"Now look at the mess I'm in," he fumed. With the head of the project at the pentagon breathing down his neck to finish the project and no one who knew enough about the chips intricate design to complete the task, Morganthau knew he was on thin ice here.

"I'm having to sit on my ass and wait for these idiots to capture Zach and bring his piss ant little ass back here to finish the job," Morganthau thought.

Morganthau knew full well that it had been his own fault. He was none-the-less ticked off at everyone who worked for him.

"When we do get him back and he finishes the project I will personally take great satisfaction in watching as my men cut out his still beating heart," he said as he broke the pencil in two with enough force to drive several splinters deep into his own hand.

Morganthau sat back in his leather chair trimmed in cherry accents and gold studded corners and swore to no one in particular. He was not accustomed to having things go so wrong.

"This was not how the plan was supposed to pan out," he thought as he picked up and slowly twirled a hand-rolled Havana Gold cigar between his mammoth fingers.

Debating between lighting the cigar and getting up to pour himself a glass of Scotch whiskey, he finally dropped the cigar on the desk and pushed his six foot-four inch frame out of the chair and walked over to the bar. He grabbed the bottle of Scotch and poured himself a shot of the golden liqueur and raised it to his lips and tossed it back in one smooth gulp.

He let out a sigh and said to himself, "best one hundred and twenty year old Scotch a man can buy."

He set the glass down on the bar and poured himself a second round, this time making it a double shot of the warm inviting liquid. He recapped the bottle and placed it back on the glass shelf at the back of the bar and walked over to one of four expansive windows that made up the east wall of his luxurious office space on the 16th floor of Technadine's headquarters.

Morganthau knew he had made a mistake this time, something he was not normally prone to doing. He should have had guards stationed at all the exits and installed those confounded security cameras in all the labs like he said he was going to do. Then he probably would have seen what Zach was up to and been able to stop him before he ran. Here he was the head of the most powerful surveillance and detection equipment manufacturing company in the world and he couldn't even keep tabs on a lowly little lab technician.

"Damn," he swore to himself again for the second time in so many minutes.

"Well, you may have outsmarted me once Zach but that's all the outsmarting you're going to be doing once my men catch up with you. And once we get you back here my friend, your lab days are all but over with."

Morganthau tossed back the double shot of Scotch with one final gulp and walked over to his desk. He set the glass down on the finely finished teakwood top and picked up the cigar. Putting the cigar to his lips he said, "Zach my boy, when we are done with you there won't be enough left of you even a dentist could recognize."

Chapter 9

July 21,2000
3:15 p.m.
Huntsville, Texas headed North on Interstate 45 to Dallas

Jamie worked on the scratches on her face using the passenger vanity mirror behind the sun visor, wincing as she applied the peroxide to each of the cuts that had been inflicted by the big mans fingernails.

"How are you doing?" Zach ask, after a few minutes had gone by since they left the grocery store. Jamie flashed a tired smile and said, "I'll live, it could have been worse." Then thinking of Fran from the restaurant she added, "I could have been the one who got shot instead of Franny."

She began to cry; softly at first and then it seemed she could not stop crying as the awful moments of the restaurant came flooding back to her in one mad rush after another.

Zach reached out hesitantly and touched the side of her face where a tear had slowly rolled down her cheek and momentarily stopped its descent at the curve of her mouth. She reached up and took his hand in hers holding it tightly against her cheek as if for protection.

After a few minutes she let go of his hand and inhaling a deep breath she said, "what did all that stuff in the letters mean? Can he really do what he plans to with just some tiny little microchip?"

Zach looked away from the road and with a smile stared into Jamie's beautiful jade green eyes, wanting so much to kiss her at that very moment and wishing they had met under different and more normal circumstances.

He turned back to watch the road ahead and began to explain, "I designed the Hal2001 Intellichip in the Technadine labs. It's a continuation of a design I had started back in my college days at Stanford. It's been a life long dream of mine."

"I named it after my favorite movie of all time. The microchip would finally be able to do what the movie version could only pretend to do. The Hal2001 would be able to reason. The first true artificial intelligence," Zach said with pride.

"With a platform built around the new chip, the Hal2001 would be capable of learning, understanding and speaking every language known to man plus all alpha and numeric languages ever developed. With the right equipment it could respond in normal sentence structure just as if you were speaking to a real human."

"And perhaps its greatest ability of all is that it would be able to remember every detail of a conversation that was ever spoken to it. It would have total recall even greater than the human brain itself could achieve and with the right sensing equipment, as Morganthau had once suggested to me, it would be able to carry on conversations at great distances."

"They could really do all that with something as small as a microchip?" Jamie asked.

"Technology has come a long way," Zach said, thinking of his days at Stanford University where he got his start.

"What I did not know until I read the secret files was that Morganthau had never intended to use the microchips in the way that I had envisioned."

"From very early on he had planned and manipulated hundreds of scientists and lab workers into thinking that its ultimate use was for University think tanks."

"Morganthau kept the labs in the dark about what each lab was working on. He never let anyone know what the final product was and whether it was delivered or not. Work was doled out to each lab and each lab given a specific time frame to complete the work in. From there the finished product went to secret testing facilities deep within the Technadine compound and it was the last we ever saw of the equipment we helped design."

Zach, was excited now as he finally was able to talk about not only his own technological breakthrough but also what he had uncovered after hacking into the top secret computer files Morganthau had kept.

"According to the files I uncovered, Morganthau envisioned the chip being surgically implanted into the brain of a host human where it would be able to send and receive messages through the brain's own messaging nerve center via the sensing equipment also designed at Technadine."

"Is that possible?" Jamie asked.

"From what I have seen in the past thirty-six hours I'd say it is not only possible but probable," Zach said.

"From what I gathered from the documents I found the sensing equipment works much the same way a cellular phone works by bouncing a signal off of radio towers via satellites stationed around the globe. Only in the sensing equipment it picks up the electrical impulses in the human brain, literally snatching the signal out of the air. It supposedly has tremendous range capabilities, but the documents do not go in to just how great that range might be."

"Theoretically, it makes it possible for people to be able to read minds, by picking up the alpha rhythms that occur naturally in the human brain enabling the host human to literally pluck voice and pictures out of thin air from anyone he locks in on."

"The chip I designed is the processing center for the information the sensing equipment picks up. It takes the raw data retrieved by the sensing equipment and turns it into recognizable information that can be stored in the host's own brain and recalled at will."

"After I had completed the initial testing, I began to notice some rather peculiar happenings in other parts of the Technadine labs that I had suddenly been classified off limits to. Then just twelve days ago they had taken the only fully functioning chip away from me without so much as a thank you or any explanation to boot. Despite my complaints I was denied access to the other labs and on top of that was practically ordered to begin final preparation for the completion of ten more chips by the end of the week."

"I began work on the other chips but I became increasingly nervous about the secretive nature of the testing in the other parts of the lab, so I decided to investigate. When I called Chuck, the technician in the lab next to mine, the phone began making strange noises and then the line went dead. When I tried to call him back all I got was dead air. There was no dial tone or busy signal just dead air. I called the front desk and was told there was a problem with the phone system throughout the company."

"Why did you not just go over to his lab and talk to him in person?" Jamie said.

"I tried."

"I got up and headed to Chuck's lab but was stopped by security and told I could have no contact with the other technicians in the company at this time. When I asked why that was I was told to mind my own business and return to my lab immediately," Zach continued.

"Back in the lab I sat and stewed about not being allowed to contact anyone else in the other labs and decided that I would find another way to contact them. But how do I check up on them without being seen, I had thought to myself. If I had been found snooping around the labs, Morganthau's men would suspect I'm spying. I tried to email the other labs but all I got was returned mail messages saying the mail could not be delivered."

"I left the lab that evening, frustrated and angry, and headed home to my condo in a suburb just outside the valley. On my way home I had the distinct feeling that I was being followed."

"All evening I could not shake the feeling that the walls had ears and the windows of my condo had eyes. I even stepped outside and looked around a few times to see if anyone was standing in the shadows near my house. But I saw nothing. Finally I could not stand it any longer and started to go to bed."

"The moment I turned off the lights in the kitchen my eyes locked on movement just outside the French doors on the back porch of my condo. I immediately went to the doors and threw them open and stepped out into the crisp night air. I started to walk toward the side of the house and around the corner where my car sat in the driveway when a large gray cat darted around the corner and across my path. I nearly jumped out of my skin," he said.

"I started to turn and head back into the house and that is when I noticed the footprints. There were wet leafy footprints leading up to the French doors at the back of the house. I turned quickly, looking toward the shadows at the back of the yard and then I ran over to the driveway and look out into the street but there was only silence. I turned and half-ran back into the house shutting and locking the door once I was safely back inside."

"I went to the front door and made sure it was locked and then I had a thought. Morganthau was having me followed. For what purpose I could not fathom, but it sent a chill through my spine and for a moment all I could think of doing was run. The overwhelming realization that I was in grave danger hit me," Zach said as he recalled the moment and the way the cold chill ran up the side of his legs and across his chest and settled deep within the recesses of his mind.

"I stood there for some time before I had another deep realization, and that was that I had to know why."

"Then I got an idea," he continued.

"The computers in the labs were all connected to the main frame in the companies IT department. I could access the main frame and get all the information I wanted. All I had to do was hack into the system and search it for any unusual documents."

"How did you do that?" Jamie asked.

"I'm a chip designer by trade but I am also a damn good hacker," he said with a wink to Jamie.

"So, I grabbed the keys to my car and headed out the door and drove back to the offices of Technadine and headed straight to my lab and switched on my computer, and logged on to Technadine's network. Within minutes I was hacking into the heavily restricted data base through a back door and was having my computer search through thousands of documents looking for anything that referenced the Hal2001 chip or my name specifically."

"What's a back door?" Jamie asked.

"It's a way for the programmer or software designer to maintain access to a program or system they have developed at anytime without being noticed or detected. It is kind of like a locksmith making a master key to every lock he's ever installed, without the customer knowing that he did it."

"That's a little scary, knowing someone can sneak in to your place anytime they want," Jamie replied.

"Imagine how it makes companies feel who rely on network servers to store their most secret documents and designs. They can get more than a little nervous when their security has been breached."

"I'll bet," Jamie said.

"The system quickly found hundreds of documents with those perimeters, so I narrowed the field by having the computer search those files that contained anything regarding new testing procedures or operations."

"That's when I came across a new entry dated 07-17-2000," he told Jamie.

"That was just five days ago," Zach said.

"I tried to open the document but the file was password protected."

"I figured that if the files were secret enough to be coded then they must be for Morganthau's eyes only, so at first I tried Morganthau's first name and initial but it did not open. I then typed several random names and words I had heard Morganthau use a few times but still I got nowhere, until I remembered Morganthau's penchant for expensive collector cars."

"After thinking a minute or two of all the cars that I had heard Morganthau owned I began to type each name in until finally on the sixth name, a Studebaker, the screen went blank and then the document appeared before my eyes."

"When I saw the file come up I almost wet my pants from the excitement," he said a little embarrassed.

Unfolding the tattered sheets of computer paper as he drove he looked at the documents once more remembering back to the vary moment of his discovery. It read:

CLASSIFIED TOP SECRET COMMUNIQUÉ
PROJECT CODE NAME: ECHO
TO: MAJOR WINSTON DAVIS
All going as planned. Primary objective is scheduled to be completed and operational on 07/20/2000.
Army Special Surgical Teams have arrived and have already been briefed on the operation. Preparations are under way and the first installment in the host subject is to be performed on 07/19/2000. Remaining installments to be performed as soon as the remaining Hal2001 chips are complete. We expect testing to began on first subject

as early as 07/20/2000. Will advise on condition of remaining subjects
and their installment dates, as they become available.
Douglas J. Morganthau

"It was the first document that you read," Zach said. "That one along with the other two documents are the only ones I have left. The remaining files are locked in the trunk of the car back at the restaurant. I was hoping to use them to shut down Morganthau and his whole secret government operation by sending copies to the newspapers around the country."

"I printed out the documents to my local printer in the lab and headed out to my car and that is when the security team spotted me and gave chase. I managed to elude them and I have been on the run ever since. I was hoping I could stop long enough to make copies of the documents and mail a set to a news station but every time I thought I had given them the slip they found me again. I managed to get past them a few times but never for very long."

"Now, without proof, I do not know what I'm going to do. Without more hard evidence the newspapers won't even blink with interest and more than likely the government is in on it too so it will get covered up way before it reaches the general public." he said dejectedly.

"Without the rest of those documents I can not go to the news stations. And, I do not have anything concrete I can turn over to the police, at least not without some hard evidence. And I know I can not go home because Morganthau's men will be waiting for me there, so I guess I'll just keep running," he said.

Jamie leaned over and placing her head against his shoulder said, "at least you won't be alone."

After a moment of silence he continued. "I could not believe what I was reading," Zach told her.

"No wonder Morganthau had cut me out of the next phase of the project. It was because he did not want me to know what his real intentions were for the Hal2001 chip. Morganthau actually planned to implant the chips into humans in an attempt to make them some kind of telepathic-capable receiver. To what end I could only guess, until I found another document dated ten days before the one I just read by searching for documents that were addressed to Davis, the Major that Morganthau had spoke of before."

"That document detailed the planned operation, ECHO as they had called it, to send spies into other world governments implanted with the Hal2001 microchip and another component I could only venture to guess was a receiver-type device for picking up varying types and degrees of sound waves. I also found a list of names and their installation dates which I guessed to be the recipients of the chips I'm building and the dates the chips were to be installed."

"If this becomes operational there is no telling what information the government could get their hands on and what they would do with it once they got it. I'm not sure who, in addition to Morganthau and Davis, are in on this government backed plot but I bet it goes pretty far up the ladder, maybe all the way to the White House."

"That far?" Jamie questioned.

"I don't know for sure but I do know one thing, I do not want my work, my dream, used for such corrupt and underhanded dirty work. Such out and out greed to have the ultimate power."

"Why is it man always has to turn everything he touches into a power trip," Zach said.

He had begun the dream of creating an artificially intelligent system back in his early years in high school. The desire had grown as he matured into adulthood and found no one his own age he could strike up a lasting relationship with. He was always somewhat of a loner-type having been the only child of academic parents who were always on tours or speaking engagements, Zach was left with his grandparents or an uncle to be cared for.

Without other kids around Zach began to develop imaginary friends to play with, but the more they became a part of his everyday life the more he felt he was alone and began to think that one day he would make the perfect child companion. Zach wished for a companion that would always be there for you and not leave you alone to play by yourself, a playmate that would respond to your questions, your feelings, not made up from the depths of your own mind.

As he grew older, his need for companionship decreased but his ideas of creating artificial intelligence continued to grow. Zach found himself reading everything on the subject of computers and artificial intelligence. His room was littered with Popular Mechanics and Popular Science magazines. His closet was a virtual library of the latest scientific books and magazines of the day. His dreams and passions had driven him up to now but they had also placed him in immediate danger and if he did not find a way out soon they would ultimately destroy him.

He did not want his dream destroyed, or worse, used for someone else's gain so he decided then and there to stop it.

"It was then I decided I had to find a way to stop Morganthau."

"But how do I stop it?" he said, again reliving the moment in his lab several days before.

"What did you do to the chips," Jamie asked.

"Before I left the lab that night I got an idea to lock out the major functions of the chips capabilities by using a back door password only I know," Zach said.

"But can someone else find it who is an equally good hacker," she ask.

"Yes, but they have to first find the word and then they have to move it to a preprogrammed unlock position and then along with the word they must type the word's definition as well. The chances are slim that any of the idiots that Morganthau hired before me will be smart enough to find it in the first place or if they do, to make all the right sequences of connections to unlock it," he said. "And besides, even if they get that far no one but myself knows what the switching sequence within the chips are and I've made certain that there are many combinations, trillions to be exact."

"It took awhile to make the modifications to all the chips, once I completed the task I headed for my car and that is when they spotted me and gave chase."

"Well, it sounds like it will take them awhile to figure it out, if ever, and in the meantime we can think of a way to expose them to the world," Jamie said laying her head back against Zach's shoulder as he drove on through the white hot afternoon.

Chapter 10

July 21, 2000
3:45 p.m.
Technadine Corporation, Silicon Valley, California

After replacing the receiver of the phone back on its hook, Morganthau got up from his desk and went to his private bar that was concealed behind a wall on the far side of his office. He poured himself a tall glass of Jack Daniel's straight up and then tossed in a couple of cubes of ice for the hell of it.

He had just gotten his ass chewed out by Major Davis because he was behind schedule and the elections were looming closer and closer for several of the countries where they planned to infiltrate those governments. Davis went on to stress how important it was that the operatives be in place in order to influence the right people within that government into electing the right man for the job.

When Morganthau hung up the phone he was on fire with anger. An anger he had not known since his father had been alive. Morganthau had been raised an only child by a military family, moving constantly from one base to another. His father, an officer in the Army and an abusive drunk, would regularly take to beating Douglas whenever he stepped over the line.

"All I had to do was breath," Morganthau thought.

Morganthau hated his parents and swore that he'd one day kill his father, but that pleasure was denied him because on his seventeenth birthday both of his parents were killed in a terrible car accident while coming home from an officer's party. They had been drinking heavily and his dad had passed out at the wheel as the car veered over into on-coming traffic and was struck head-on by an eighteen wheeler loaded down with auto parts. The small sports car they were driving never had a chance and what remained of the bodies would not have filled a cigar box.

Not that Morganthau cared. He did not even attend the funeral. He just packed up his things and left that day taking some money and jewelry that had been stashed in a sock drawer in his parent's bedroom.

Douglas had been on the street less than a month before he was arrested on burglary charges. The judge, a fat, cigar smoking old fart gave him a choice, "either join the service or spend the next five years in the state penitentiary."

Douglas opted for the Army, not because he thought it would be easier, but it suddenly occurred to him how much damage he could do to his parent's good military names. It did not take long though for him to realize that he liked being in the military, hell, he loved it. And before long he had been given a promotion and sent to numerous schools all over the country, paid for by good old Uncle Sam no less.

He was liked by all of his parent's old friends and quickly became a regular at some of the highest level meetings and talks on the current situation in Vietnam. When he asked to be sent over to Vietnam, his friends in the top brass said no. He eventually convinced them that it would be, militarily and politically speaking, a good career move for him and with some congratulations he was given command of a platoon and sent "in country."

His platoon hit it off from the start, like they were parts of some perfectly built killing machine. They quickly became known as silent terrors of the jungle. Able to strike at anytime, day or night, without ever tipping off the enemy that they were there until it was too late. Then something happened. They became bored with fighting just the North Vietcong and took to hunting, stalking any platoon, enemy or friendly, as if they were animals searching for their prey.

Some said that the government was behind it and knew all along what the platoon was doing deep in the jungles. They accused the military of experimenting with mind-altering drugs in order to create the ultimate fighting machine. But things started to go wrong with the platoon. The Army lost track of them in the jungles of Vietnam and it was not until reports of mass destruction of villages and enemy patrols that the Army knew where they had been.

They finally caught up with them, but it was too late for one village. The platoon had surprised a relatively large village in the western province and slowly and methodically wiped out every last man, woman and child. The people of the village had no idea what was happening to them but they were systematically killed and skinned over the course of a week's time.

The neighboring villagers soon started calling the attacks the Night Killer because all the attacks occurred at night, and the only way the village knew something had happened is when they awoke several people of the village were found hanging from trees, skinned alive. The Army finally captured the platoon and the whole unit was put on trial but the Army did not want it leaking to the outside world so it was hushed. After the trial nothing was ever said about the platoon again.

The whole platoon was transferred to a facility in the States and underwent exhaustive testing over the course of two years to determine the extent and range of their physic abilities but they were eventually released. The men had secretly decided to act dumb about their special skills and said the killings were done out of boredom.

Morganthau had been exonerated of any wrong doing and had been re-assigned to another command. Morganthau had been trained in communications during the war and had become particularly interested in the latest developments in the surveillance and detection field. Because of his connections high up in the military and the political arena, he was given special clearance to use and experiment with new communications capabilities.

Some say that is why the platoon, which consisted of only sixteen men, could sneak up on and wipe out an entire enemy patrol of more than seventy-five men and quietly disappear back into the jungle without ever being notice or seen and not just once but numerous times.

Through the help of some political cronies and because of his close military ties and background in communication, Morganthau quietly retired from the military and was hired on at Technadine Corporation as a communications liaison to oversee the military applications division of the company.

Technadine Corporation was founded just after the Second World War. Its primary claim to fame was the development of the most sophisticated surveillance and detection devices known to man. The company was secretly financed by the government to help develop new ways of detecting enemy positions during wartime and if possible, during peace time as well.

With the government's backing, Technadine had developed an endless assortment of high-tech gadgetry that would make Agent 007 jealous, including several low earth orbit spy satellites that were aimed over some nasty Middle Eastern countries and were still being used by the government today.

Ten years later and a steady climb up the corporate ladder, no doubt with more help from his pals in the military, Morganthau had become the President and CEO of Technadine Corporation. Less than a year later he had removed all of the few board members remaining who did not see things his way and had surrounded himself with his old Vietnam buddies.

Ever since his days spent in the Army's communication labs, Morganthau had envisioned a new type of motion detection and sensing equipment. Equipment so small that it could be implanted into a person's body and used like a homing device, able to track and lock on movement from anywhere around that person for up to 100 kilometers.

But what he was now attempting to develop was beyond even his wildest fantasy. A new breed of sensory preceptor microchip that would be implanted into the brain of specially trained operatives and they, in turn, would be strategically placed high up in all the key governments of the world including, unbeknownst to his trusted cohorts, the US Government.

It was, as Morganthau planned, to gain what he quietly thought of as the ultimate power for himself. With information like that he would be able to control world talks and hold whole countries for ransom to the highest bidder. And with his special team of maniac loyalists beside him, he could never be touched.

Immediately after Morganthau had rid himself of the "soft under belly" of the company, as he like to call the old board members, he had amassed a legion of cut throat marketing and scientific strategist to start work on the ultimate weapon. With help from the US Government and an unlimited supply of financial support thanks to a secret Government fund, Morganthau began development on the new chip. But the work was slow and the top brass were breathing down his neck to see some results, so when development began to stall Morganthau decided to look for some new blood in the scientific field to help complete the puzzle that was just beyond his grasp.

He found Zach Denton, a brilliant young chip designer working at one of the smaller Silicon Valley firms stamping out chips at a dime a dozen. After talking to him about the new chip, staying clear of its real purpose, he had decided that Zach was the man for the job.

Morganthau promised him a sizable income and a condo in one of the nicest areas of Silicon Valley. Zach could not resist. Within three months Morganthau's new acquisition to the team had completely redesigned and reprogrammed the chip, breaking new ground in chip technology that none of the other firms had even come close to considering.

"But he evidently got suspicious when we went to the next phase of our testing and started snooping around looking for clues," Morganthau thought to himself. "Well, when we get him back this time he will not have a chance in hell of escaping until after the work is completed and then the only way he's leaving this fucking compound is in a body bag," Morganthau hissed.

Chapter 11

Whiteslayer and Jake stopped at a diner to grab a bite to eat. They had been chasing Zach for thirty-six hours non-stop now. They should of had him back at the restaurant in Houston and if it were not for the girl and for the fact that Zach never stopped to eat or sleep those first three days, they would have been back at the compound by now enjoying themselves.

But Whiteslayer was confident now, more confident than he had been since they started out after him. He could feel the connection he had made with Zach. It was like an extra beating heart inside his head. At first the feeling had overwhelmed him and made him claustrophobic. He wanted to tear the device out of his head and rip it to shreds, but gradually the feeling subsided and now, now it was magic. He felt he was alive with energy, like he was stealing the very essence of the souls from the people he locked in on.

There were limitations, he knew that, the power was still not quite perfected because he would lose the connection from time to time like you would lose a radio station as you drove through the mountains, only to pick it up again once you got to the other side.

Jake wasn't talking and it was fine with Whiteslayer as they sat and ate in silence. He did not care much for the big man and had even less respect for him since he had gained so much weight and let himself go. Whiteslayer had no respect for anyone who abused his or her own bodies. "The body is my temple, there is no god but that which I make of myself," he would tell anyone who cared to listen.

He suddenly stopped in mid-thought and pounding the table he stood, making the other patrons in the diner look up with a start.

"Come on," he said to Jake, "I've lost the signal," and turned and walked out into the late afternoon sun.

Jake quickly threw some money onto the counter and grabbing a last bite of his burger, hurried for the door.

Chapter 12

July 21, 2000
5:00 p.m.
Driving through Dallas, heading for the north side of town and
D/FW Airport.

After driving around Dallas for awhile, Zach and Jamie decided to continue driving until they reached Fort Worth, Texas. For several hours they drove around the once small Texas cow-town looking at the sites as they wasted time, not wanting to stop for fear it was still too early in the day and they might be spotted. Zach was not sure how Whiteslayer had been able to find him so fast at the restaurant.

"Surely they hadn't implanted the chip so soon into a host and made it operational yet," he thought.

His mind did not want to believe it but his heart said they had indeed been able to do as Morganthau had planned. Someone who was more than just evil was now chasing Zach. He was almost super-human.

Passing through downtown Fort Worth was like going back in time, Zach thought as he drove by one massive stone building after another obviously built in the city's heyday as a livestock center. The subdivisions that had cropped up in and around downtown were of every age and class make-up imaginable. It was easy to see the progression of the city's growth as you passed from simple wood frame track homes of the forties and fifties to pink brick and stucco structures of the sixties and seventies. Continuing growth was evident by the modern two story all brick homes complete with detached garage and porte cochere that had begun to spring up replacing the older homes once the pride of a new home owner.

It was testament to humankind's ability to adapt to change, to thrive in the wake of an ever-evolving world.

They had agreed that it would be best if they waited as long as possible before doubling back and stopping in Dallas for the night at the first hotel that didn't look too conspicuous. They had both hesitantly agreed that it would be almost impossible for Morganthau's men to find them for at least a day maybe even several days. They hoped to be thousands of miles away by then, sipping on frozen daiquiris and lounging beside a pool in some remote island paradise.

Zach secretly knew that if they found him as quick once they could surely find him just as easily a second time. He did not let on to Jamie because he did not want to scare her more than she already was scared.

It was almost ten thirty in the evening when they made their way back to Dallas and stopped at a Mexican Restaurant to get some take out and then checked into a motel a couple of miles from the freeway. Zach pulled up next to the lobby of the Star Bright Motel in the night shrouded shadows of an old dilapidated awning that hung along the front and down most of one side of the motel's parking area. The rest of the awning, Zach noticed, had long ago seen its last days and all that remained were a couple of rusted poles still protruding from the badly cracked asphalt of the unkempt parking lot like some emaciated sentinels of a long since forgotten fort.

*   *   *

While Zach went in to pay, Jamie sat in the car looking out at the parking lot and the mostly empty motel rooms. She too saw the poles of the awning standing in their silent vigil outside the rooms and thought how the light from the motel cast an eerie light on the poles making it seem as though they were bleeding from wounds received in some long ago battle. She knew it was only the rust from years of neglect but still it sent a chill right through her settling deep into her bones.

*   *   *

Zach paid with what little cash he had left on him telling the night manager that they would only be staying the one night. The manager, an old leather faced man of about sixty stood a good foot and a half taller than Zach. Now, because of numerous injuries from more than a few falls from his days riding bareback competition at rodeos all over Texas and several other states, it was all he could do to look eye to eye at Zach.

"Don't reckon I care one lick how long you stay so long as you pay me now," the man said.

Without replying, Zach picked up the keys the night manager had thrown on the counter and turned and walked out the door. He drove over to the far end of the parking lot where the awning was still standing, parking beside a an old GMC pickup truck that looked like it had not moved in twenty years. Zach noted with a chuckle that it appeared that they had poured asphalt right around the truck with out bothering to even move it.

Jamie and Zach got out of the car and walked over to the stairs that led up to the second floor room, No. 215, midway down the line of run down looking rooms. They had requested a room on the second floor and in the center of the U-shaped complex so that Zach would be able to see everyone that came and went as he looked out the window of the room.

While eating the take out dinners at the small wobbly table that served as the dining area of their tiny motel room they discussed their next plans.

"I think it would be best if we take the first flight out in the morning out of the Dallas/Fort Worth Airport, it's not far away, in fact I saw the signs as we drove around tonight," Zach said.

"I agree, but where do we go?" Jamie asks.

"First to Florida just long enough to make the necessary arrangements for passports and such, and then to some Caribbean island where I figure we can wire my bank for money to handle living expenses, for awhile anyway," Zach replied.

Zach was not rich but he had saved quite a bit of money over the years and now had a sizable savings account to draw from in case of emergencies. He knew that if ever there were an emergency this would qualify.

D/FW airport was not far from their motel and they figured they could get up early and go to the airport and wait for their flight, making reservations in Jamie's name just in case Whiteslayer went looking for Zach at the airport.

"But what if they find us before then? What if they track us to this location before we can leave and get to the airport?" Jamie said.

She was shaking again, remembering the horrible scene at the restaurant. Zach stood and went to her side and wrapping his arms around her let her bury her face into his shoulder gently caressing her as she started to cry.

"It will be all right, I promise," he said as he pushed the hair from her face and gave her a soft kiss on the forehead.

She looked up with those glistening green eyes and Zach knew he was in love. For the first time in his life Zach Denton knew what it was like to actually be in love, and he liked it. He was also aware that he was more frightened of what the future held for them than he had ever been in his whole life.

Chapter 13

July 21, 2000
6:15 p.m.
East Side of Downtown Dallas, Texas

"They must have decided to continue right past Dallas and head for the Arkansas line," Whiteslayer said, as he and Jake climbed into the van and tore out of the parking lot, quickly entering the freeway headed for Dallas.

Whiteslayer had lost all signals from Zach but yet, felt that both Zach and the girl were not very far away and had no plans to try to make it to the bordering state. When they reached Dallas, Whiteslayer had once again picked up Zach's thoughts but because of the tall buildings that dotted the Dallas skyline could not keep him locked in.

Again the radio effect of fading in and out had made it too difficult to concentrate without causing a major throbbing sensation to occur at the base of his skull. Twice as they drove toward the looming skyline Whiteslayer had to tell Jake to pull over to the side of the road because he had become violently ill from the effects.

Whiteslayer and Jake drove completely around Dallas trying to get a fix on Zach's location and then headed for Fort Worth when he once again picked up the signal. The continual concentration plus the radio effects that constantly plagued Whiteslayer forced him to stop trying to hold the signal for more than a few seconds at a time. After following

Zach around Fort Worth for over two hours Whiteslayer decided to pull over to the side of the road and wait for Zach's next move.

Two more hours went by when Whiteslayer opened his eyes with a start and turned to Jake who had fallen asleep in the drivers seat and was snoring loudly, the sound echoing off the walls of the van, reached out and punched the big man in the arm.

"Wake up and drive," Whiteslayer said with a scowl.

Irritable that he had been awakened from a pleasant dream, Jake started the engine and threw it into gear leaving a trail of smoke from the tires as he left the parking lot of the boarded up filling station where he had parked the van earlier. They made two complete searches of the city and were about to make a third when Whiteslayer finally located the motel Zach and the girl had stopped at. It was several blocks off the freeway nestled in some tall pines and surrounded by a tall metal fence that looked to be at least twelve feet tall and covered with ivy.

"The fence must have been partially concealing Zach's signal," he said more to himself than to Jake who was still pissed that he had been jolted out of such a great nap.

They pulled into the parking lot and drove around to the side of the building behind the office, out of site from the view each of the motel rooms shared of the motel parking lot. Jake started to get out of the van but Whiteslayer stopped him.

"Stay," Whiteslayer said, "we're going to let them think they lost us, give them a chance to relax and let their guard down." "We'll bunk down in the van for the night and wait till morning to take him."

Chapter 14

July 21, 2000
10:15 p.m.
Star Bright Motel, northwest side of Dallas

After eating, Jamie and Zach lay on the bed talking and making plans. Zach reached over and picked up the 9mm that he had earlier placed on the night table by the bed and handed it to Jamie.

"What do you want me to do with that?" she asked.

"I want you to keep an eye on the parking lot. If anything looks suspicious you come tell me."

"Where are you going?" she ask, suddenly afraid that Zach is planning to leave her here alone.

Noting the concern in her voice, Zach reached out and placed his hand to her cheek and said, "don't worry. I'm just going to go and take a shower, it's been awhile since this old body of mine has felt clean and I'd like to do something about it."

Zach gets up off the bed feeling a little tired and a lot sore. The muscles in his back sending a message to his brain that he had spent way to much time in a sitting position as he raced across the Southwestern United States in his once pristine Ford Mustang. For a brief moment he wondered what would become of his beloved car that he had left behind at the restaurant, but only briefly. He was more eager to climb into a hot shower and scrub away some of the aches than worry about the past and some old worldly possession. Besides, what worried him the most was what the future held for him and how he was going to get out of this mess he was in. He also worried for Jamie. But he quickly turned his face away from her as he headed toward the bathroom, so as not to let her catch the worry in his expression.

*   *   *

While Zach took a shower, Jamie pulled a chair up close to the window and sat down. With a nervous sigh she pulled back the old worn curtain and hesitantly peered out into the parking lot but could see no one.

"The place looks deserted," she spoke softly to herself.

The night had fallen over the dilapidated old motel and it's broken down awning like a death shroud. Jamie shook off the gloomy thought and tried to replace it with something a little more pleasant. She remembered back over the course of the day when Zach had first walked into the restaurant, how he had stared at her through piercing blue eyes and what he had said under his breath.

"Did he really want her?" she thought.

"Does he really think I'm beautiful?"

Jamie had not heard anyone tell her she was pretty since her father said it so many years before. She never thought of herself as such and certainly did not think anyone else did. She had grown up in the country, rarely wearing anything but blue jeans and boots. The only time she dressed up was for church on Sundays and that was usually by force. Her Momma insisted that she, "look like a lady, even if you don't feel like one." She did not like getting all fixed up and absolutely hated make-up. It always made her face feel dirty and she would wipe it off after wearing it only a short time. The only reason she wore dresses at all now was because the manager of the restaurant where she worked insisted that she dress nice for the patrons.

"More like animals than people," she thought to herself.

She sat looking out the window of the motel room and wondering what her mom was doing right now. She had not been home much in the past year, ever since her mom had remarried. After her father had died her mother had taken to spending the evenings at the local honky-tonk in town and would regularly bring home strange men, but none of them seemed to stay long. Jamie had to fight off more than a few of her mom's boyfriends who had taken a perverted interest in her.

Once, while she was in the shower, one of them had walked in on her in the middle of shampooing her hair and had grabbed her between the legs. While her mom had gone to the store to pick up some groceries for dinner he had stripped off his clothes and strolled into the bathroom with a huge hard-on and a big grin on his face.

"I know you been watching me and wishing it was you I was doing it to, so now's your chance," he had said as he put one foot into the tub, still holding her crotch.

She was so shocked she had been unable to speak, which he instantly picked up on as a sign that it was ok to continue, and started to climb the rest of the way into the shower with her. She finally came out of her shock then and threw soap in his eyes and pushed him backward over the commode and into the counter top where his head connected with a dull thud. He hit the floor like a sack of potatoes, blood streaming from the gash to the back of his head. She ran from the shower and into her father's old study and grabbed a shotgun off the display rack behind his desk, pointing it at the doorway just as the man half-ran, half-stumbled into the room.

He stopped when he saw the shotgun pointed at him and said, "come on now, you wouldn't want to hurt me would you? All I wanted to do was satisfy that hunger I seen in your eyes," he said in a backwoods country drawl.

She had been so frightened, she did not know if she could pull the trigger. But as he started to walk towards her she instinctively lowered the barrel of the gun till she was aiming at his now shrunken member.

"If you want to find out what its like to be a girl just you come a little closer and I'll blow your pecker clean off," she said.

He quickly reached for his penis as if that would protect it from a bullet and said, "you fucking bitch! I was only trying to do you a favor since you was so homely looking and all. I knew you was never going to get a man the honest way."

He turned and headed for her mother's bedroom, grabbing his clothes and running out the front door of the house without even bothering to stop and get dressed. Jamie sat down in a chair that looked out on the front yard of the house and watched as he jumped in his truck and sped off and then she started to cry.

It was the same chair her dad had sat in every evening to read his newspaper or at night with her in his lap would read her a bedtime story. She was still sitting in the chair, naked, holding the shotgun and crying when her mother got home and she told her what had happened. Thinking that her mom would console her, she was unprepared for the verbal lashing her mother launched into. She could not believe her mom had accused her of trying to steal her boyfriend away from her and denying her the only pleasure she had left in the world. Then her mom had slapped her across the face and stormed out of the room, leaving her more confused and upset than she had ever been in her life.

"God, I have got to get out of here!" she remembered thinking.

But it was not until five months later after Jamie turned eighteen, and her mom had just married the deacon of their church, that she packed up her things and left home. She could not stand the preacher's sermonizing anymore than the constant battles her and her mother had on a daily basis.

So with the car her dad had giving her just before his death on her fifteenth birthday and a small portion of her inheritance that she had received after his death, the rest of the inheritance would be giving to her on her twenty-first birthday, she headed for Houston, Texas.

She quickly found an apartment in the area known as Montrose and began looking for a job in the want ads of the local newspaper. Finding a job proved to be harder than she thought because no one wanted to hire an inexperienced eighteen-year-old fresh from the farm. She had finally been hired on at "The Stables Eatery" restaurant as a waitress/hostess and had been there ever since.

"At least until now," she thought, as she looked out the dirty window and into the gloomy night beyond. Now she didn't know what she was going to do or what the future held for her.

*   *   *

Zach stood for what seemed like hours under the hot pulsating stream of water. He had not felt this relieved in quite some time now and he did not want to spoil the moment. The past forty-eight hours had been the worst he had ever been through and he hoped and prayed it would be his last. But he was kidding himself. As long as Whiteslayer was looking for him and had that chip in his head then Zach was going to be hunted until they found him.

"How did I manage to get myself into such a mess," he thought.

He began to think about his University days and of his late parents and how he missed them. It had been years since they had died but he could still remember how he had felt when they told him that they were separating, and how he had stopped talking to either of his parents after their divorce. He had been angry towards both of them for breaking up, especially after staying together through so many years of hard times, before both finally making names for themselves in the academic community.

Zach's parents had both been professors at the University of Ohio when they had fallen in love and married in '66. Zach had been born two years later and had immediately shown signs of exceptional abilities early on in his child development. His father, having been a professor of Physics and his mother, an English professor, Zach had been surrounded by books of higher learning from the time he was able to walk and talk.

By the time Zach reached three years old he was talking at the junior high school level and by age five could speak French as well as English. His parents enrolled him in a school for gifted children and he quickly proved his superior intelligence by beating kids twice his age at games of Chess and other school activities.

But all was not great at home, his parents spent more and more time away from Zach, as each went their separate ways to lecture and give speeches at other universities and government functions. Zach was increasingly left behind with friends or relatives and he started to develop imaginary relationships with non-existent playmates. It was then that he had the idea to create an artificially intelligent playmate, one that would not leave him and would always be there for him.

Zach finished high school at the age of ten and was enrolled in college the next year. He went on to major in Physics and foreign languages at the University of Ohio. Then he was lured away to the prestigious campus of Stanford University in the fall of '84. At the ripe old age of sixteen he entered Stanford to study electrical engineering.

In '86 his dad sent word to him that his mother had died from breast cancer and he had briefly returned home for the funeral and to help his dad take care of her belongings. Zach tried to talk to his dad and to catch up on what his mom and dad had been doing all of the years that Zach had been away, but his father just sat in his leather easy chair and stared off into the distance as if Zach wasn't there.

As a child Zach could never seem to get his parents attention and he could see that time hadn't changed things much. Zach finally packed up to head back to school in California. He left his dad sitting in that same old chair without saying a single word to him as he walked out the door.

Two years later he received a phone call from a family friend that his dad had passed away sitting in that very same chair. He had had a heart attack and they had found him a few days later when he failed to show for a speaking engagement.

It wasn't until he settled at Stanford that he began his life-long dream of designing microchips and working in the field of artificial intelligence. Without family to return to in Ohio, Stanford University became his family and he became well known on campus and highly respected. While at Stanford he immersed himself in the study of robotics and won numerous awards before finally leaving academic life for the more lucrative side of private industry. He found himself less than happy though, moving from one company to the next without realizing his dream.

Companies were reluctant to give such a young scientist the necessary freedom to explore new avenues of science and he was relegated to modernizing gaming platforms for the latest game-makers.

Disappointed and thinking seriously about returning to academia, he was hired on at a small microchip design firm and was given free rein over his work. He began making new headway in his designs and took the computer industry by storm with his discovery of the copper-based micron RISC chip. It was not long after that Morganthau got wind of his success and offered him the job at Technadine.

In the beginning he was welcomed with open arms and given all the latest in high-tech equipment and the absolute perfect lab. He was given an enormous budget and free rein to develop his designs. It seemed that he had finally made it to the top of his career goals and was embarking on a new and rewarding life. He had no idea that he would one day find himself on the run from his employer and in fear for his life.

With the thought still lingering on his brain he let out a soft sigh and reached down and turned off the water. The water slowed to a trickle but refused to quit altogether, it's constant drip-drip-drip from the shower head resounded off the tub's spigot making a hollow clinking sound as water met metal. Zach stared for several seconds at the water's continued assault before finally reaching for the towel that hung from the shower curtain rod. He pressed the soft cotton towel into his face, wiping away the water, and at the same time seeming to, hoping to wipe away the past thirty-six hours as if it were nothing more than dirt from the road.

Zach actually looked down at the towel as he pulled it from his face, half expecting to see a dirty imprint of his face in the towel. The towel was as clean as when he hung it over the curtain rod, which was like saying that the Star Bright Motel was a five-star establishment. He ran the towel over the rest of his body, only half trying to dry himself, and then wrapped the towel around his waist and stepped from the shower.

*   *   *

Jamie turned as Zach emerged from the shower, a towel wrapped around his waist, his hair still damp but combed neatly back from his face. Jamie watched as he approached her, drops of water running from his hair and down his shoulders to mingle in the hairs on his chest. She was becoming aroused at the site of him standing there, his skin glistening in the dim light of the room.

"It's your turn in the shower," Zach said, snapping her out of the trance she had slipped into.

"I'm afraid they will come and get you while I'm in the shower and I will never see you again," she said, standing and moving into the protective embrace of his arms.

Zach lifted her chin and kissed her lightly on the lips and said, "you can leave the door open while you shower, I promise, I won't look."

*   *   *

As Jamie slipped from his arms Zach turned his back to her and looked out the window so she could undress herself. He turned around only when he heard the shower curtain close as she steps into the now steaming water. He could imagine her wet body and how the water must look as it cascades over the soft curves of her breast and then down between the soft flesh of her thighs.

It has been a long time since he has been with a woman, never seeming to have the time to develop a lasting relationship with someone. His job and his life's ambitions had always taken priority in his life over everything else. His last attempt at a relationship ended rather abruptly when the girl he had been dating had given up waiting for him to come home nights. She had nailed a goodbye letter to the keyboard of his home computer, driving the nail right through the center of the "Return" key on the keyboard. He was fast becoming a lifetime bachelor.

Zach heard the shower shut off and the curtain being pulled open. He thought about how beautiful she looked when he first laid eyes on her back at the restaurant and wondered if maybe they had a chance at a real relationship.

"If I am lucky enough to get out of this mess I'm in I will do whatever it takes to get that chance," Zach thought.

*　　　　　*　　　　　*

Jamie slipped out of her dress that she had been wearing when all of this began. She was unaccustomed to undressing in the same room with a man but Zach was being a gentleman by keeping his back to her so she could have some privacy without shutting the door. Jamie stepped into the shower and let the warm water cascade over her shoulders. Jamie thought of Zach as she applied soap to her skin moving the bar of soap over her breasts and down her chest to the small forest-like thatch between her legs realizing that she had become increasingly aroused as she bathed. Her thoughts constantly returning to the drops of water that glistened as they ran down the front of Zach's chest.

She wondered if Zach was the one. The guy she was destined to fall in love with and marry. She certainly thought he was cute enough and he seemed to Jamie to be trusting and caring. She found that he had a lot of the same characteristics her dad had. He was soft spoken, rugged good looks, but not too good-looking, sincere and trusting and just a little bit cocky. Especially when he talked about his work.

Jamie remembered how her dad had always talked about his work and the things he'd seen and the places he'd been. She would sit and listen to him for hours, as he would talk about all of the places his work had taken him and how other cultures lived. Jamie loved to listen to her dad and the stories he would tell her. It was the thing she missed most about her dad.

Jamie turned off the shower and grabbed the towel from the towel bar by the shower curtain. She dried herself off and wrapped the towel around her, tucking it in tight across her breast. She stopped and looked in the dilapidated old mirror that hung slightly crocked over the sink that was covered with stains left by years of neglect and abuse. She stared back at her reflection and wondered if she had done the right thing by running with Zach. She hardly knew the guy and here she was standing in the bathroom of a motel room with a total stranger in the next room.

"How did this happen?" She thought. "How did I end up here with a total stranger?"

She wanted to believe Zach was in trouble and needed her help. She wanted to believe that there was something there between them, a spark, and a hidden force that had pulled them together. Maybe it was destiny that had brought them together or maybe fate. Whatever it was, Jamie knew one thing for sure, that Zach was a special person and if given the chance she wanted to find out where this was all going to lead. She also knew one other thing, and that was that she had desires and needs and this was the first time in her life that she felt this strongly about any one person.

For once in her life Jamie was ready and willing to take a chance. To jump in with both feet and see where the tide took her. Jamie looked deep into the image reflected in the mirror, took a deep breath of air and said, "it's time to take the plunge girlfriend."

With that she walked from the bathroom to where Zach was standing by the window, staring out into the night-shrouded parking lot. With a gentle hand on his arm, she turned Zach around to look into her eyes. Jamie looked into Zach's tired but wanting eyes and saw a man who is both a mystery and yet somehow familiar. Like they could have known each other all their lives but only in passing. Never really having met but both aware of the others presence.

Their faces are now so close Zach can smell the shampoo in her hair. "It's like being in the middle of a rose garden," Zach thought.

"I've never been with a man before," she says as she leans forward and kisses him first a hesitant gentle kiss and then more deeply, with all the passion bubbling up within a twenty year old virgin.

Jamie takes Zach's hand and leads him to the bed and hands him a small bottle of baby oil that she had Zach purchase at the store earlier in the day.

"I always rub baby oil in my skin after I take a shower, it helps to keep my skin soft," she tells him.

"Would you rub some on my back for me," she says as she pulls apart the towel wrapped around her to reveal her nakedness.

Zach watches as it falls to the floor around her feet. "She is more beautiful than I could ever have imagined," he thinks as he stares at the wonder before him.

Her breasts are not large but nor are they small. They are well proportioned to the rest of her body, which glistens from the dampness of the shower. She has broad shoulders, as if she might have been on a school swim team in her high school days, with firm looking arms that are tight but not too muscular. Below her breasts is a grid-work of muscles and rib cage.

"She has definitely tried to keep herself in shape," Zach thinks as his eyes take in the beauty before him.

Jamie lies down on the bed, and watches as Zach removes his own towel from his waist revealing his manhood. She has only seen the male penis a few times in her young life. That one time when her mom's boyfriend tried to get too friendly and once when her and her girlfriend had gone to Galveston to go swimming and of course to look at boys.

A cute guy was playing flag football with a bunch of other guys on the beach when he leaped in the air to catch the ball. A guy on the other team had grabbed him around the waist to pull him down and the cute guy's bathing suit had nearly come completely off. Jamie and her girl-friend both sat wide-eyed looking at this enormous penis just twelve feet away. The guy stood up with his swimsuit around his ankles and looked at them, and then down at his member and turned beet red. He quickly hitched up his suit and muttered an apology then sprinted in the direction of the culprit who caused the embarrassing moment no doubt to inflict a certain amount of deserved pain on the guy.

Jamie and her girlfriend were too busy laughing hysterically with their faces buried in their beach towels to see what had become of the other guy. About that time her girlfriend's mom had come out to where they lay and informed them it was time to get back so they never got to scc the cute guy again. No doubt her mom had seen the whole thing too but never once mentioned it to either of them.

*   *   *

Zach positioned himself on the bed next to Jamie. He opened the bottle of baby oil and slowly poured oil down her back and began to caress the slippery liquid into her skin, first massaging the oil into her shoulders, down her back and finally to the soft white flesh of her buttocks.

Jamie turns over and taking his hand in hers she brings it to her lips and gently kisses each of Zach's fingers before guiding his hand to her breast. He is instantly excited by the firmness of her nipples as he pours out more of the oil from the bottle, down the front of her body, letting it dribble out over one nipple and then the other, then moving down her chest to the navel where it pools. He rubs the baby oil into her skin, first rubbing into the chest and nipples and then down her belly, over the arms and on the neck. He has her raise each leg and slowly massages them down with the oil.

"I have never known this kind of pleasure," she thinks to herself, mesmerized by the feeling that has come over her. It feels so good.

Zach bends down and gently kisses her just below the left ear as she pats the bed next to her and says, "lay next to me."

He spreads out beside her and without a word Jamie takes the bottle of oil and pours some of the clear slippery liquid into the palm of her hand and starts to rub it into his skin, hesitantly at first, but with each successive stroke she becomes more confident. She becomes excited by his response as she lightly brushes her hand against his maleness as she caresses the oil deep into his skin. They lay together; gently touching and stroking each other until the oil has absorbed into their bodies and only the scent of it is left to linger around them.

Wrapped in a tight embrace, Zach kisses her a long deep kiss. Jamie responds with a breathless moan. Zach moves down her neck planting small kisses as he goes and reaching her breasts takes each of her firm nipples in his mouth and sucks and licks them till the nipples become hard, and ache to the touch. She reaches for the burning hot shaft pressed against the flesh of her leg and begins to rub his now aching member, running her fingers over the tip and then stroking it in long slow strokes. Zach has moved his own hand to the gently folds between her legs caressing her, guiding his fingers deep inside her.

Time seems to stand still as they silently kiss and explore the boundaries of each other's bodies sometimes playfully, sometimes passionately but with excited pleasure that grows with every caress. From time to time they embrace and hold each other tightly, each one of them afraid that if they let go they will surely lose the other forever.

After a short time Zach begins to feel the wanting in her, as their caresses become more urgent, more demanding. He moves over her, gently kissing her firm nipples as he works his way down to her belly button where he pauses and slowly circles the small indentation of her navel with his tongue. Jamie spreads her legs as he moves down between them welcoming him to her. Her hands at her side, she grabs up the sheet they lay upon clenching it tightly, as if she were afraid that she would rise off the bed and float away were it not for her death grip upon the sheet.

He has begun to ache with anticipation as he imagines how it will feel when he finally enters her and they become as one in that final grand union, the ultimate embrace.

*   *   *

Zach never considered himself a good lover. His mind was always preoccupied with his work to take much more than a passing interest in dating, sex and relationships. Which was exactly why he was still a bachelor at thirty-three years old. He sometimes saw other couples around campus cuddling and holding each other and kissing and sometimes he longed to have a serious relationship but, with his projects at the university taking so much of his precious time, he could never seem to find an opportunity to explore a meaningful relationship.

The few times he did manage to get involved with a woman usually ended in disaster. And more often than not he just didn't have the same feelings for the girl as they had for him. There always seemed to be something missing in every relationship he had. Call it bad Karma or, whatever you want, it just wasn't there for him. And so he usually ended the relationship after only a few weeks of dating.

But somehow from his very first encounter with Jamie—seeing her at the restaurant touched off something deep within his mind. A sense of knowing, of some profound recognition that this person was the one. It was fate. That's the only way he could describe it. And now, to behold the sight that was before him was just amazing, it was cosmic. The feelings of pleasure and oneness he felt with her now was indescribable, it was simply the most amazing emotional experience he had ever encountered.

Zach continued to stroke and caress her, moving his hands over the firm but supple breasts, the tight muscles across her stomach, exploring her body like it was the greatest expedition he had ever been on until, after some time, Jamie cried out with climatic pleasure.

*   *   *

Jamie first rises then collapses against the pillow beneath her as if a great massive weight has been lifted from her body. She has never known pleasure of this kind before. All her life Jamie has pushed away people who wanted to get close to her. She could never bring herself to get involved even though she longed to find someone to fill the void in her life after leaving home and living on her own for so long. The few guys that asked her out since moving to Houston were too immature for her tastes. More than a few of them were down right disgusting— having so many tattoos and body piercing's that they reminded her of human pin cushions.

But when Zach walked into the restaurant and spoke for the first time to her their seemed to be an instant attraction. There was something warm and inviting hidden behind those blue eyes of his. Jamie couldn't quite put her finger on it but the feeling was one of deep understanding and commitment that instantly made her feel almost child-like and at-ease around him. Jamie couldn't quite put her finger on what attracted her to Zach but she was having no trouble expressing her feelings at this moment. She was engulfed in a passion so deep and profound that it gave her a sense of utter invincibility. She wanted to give all of herself to Zach at this very moment and hold nothing back—she felt she was making up for all the lost love and lost time of the past. She was freeing her self of the loneliness and confusion that she has felt all these many years since her dad died. It was time to let her self go, to be free, to soar.

Jamie quickly pulls him up to her and as he enters her she lets out a loud gasp of surprise at the stiffness of him.

"It feels like it's on fire," she thinks, her mind now swimming with pleasure. All of the bad times of the past, all of the day's terror are slipping away. She is lost, however, temporary in this one moment of blind animal-like passion. As their piston-like movements become more frantic, more urgent, she gives her whole self to him as she feels herself being carried away to the heavens on the wings of great white birds, soaring higher and higher till they are but one bright point of light in the sky.

Chapter 15

July 22, 2000
4:35 a.m.
Star Bright Motel, Dallas, Texas

Jamie blinks. There is a small bright light shining in her eyes as she fights to swim to the surface of what was probably the best night's sleep she has had in ages. Jamie try's to blink away the light as she fights off the grogginess of sleep.

"Jamie. Jamie, wake up," Zach is whispering to her.

"We have to go."

Jamie reaches up with both hands and wraps her arms around Zach's neck and pulls him down on top of her and kisses him deeply. Then hugging him tight to her body she says, "let's stay here forever and ever and make love again and again until we die from sheer exhaustion."

Zach kisses her softly wanting so much to hold her like this forever just as Jamie says but knowing that time is against them and that they have probably pushed their luck by stopping at this motel. He knows they have lost precious time and can't afford to waste anymore.

"We have to go, Jamie. We have to put as much distance as possible between us and Morganthau's men as we can. When I know we are truly safe then we can relax and I promise we will always be together."

"Do you promise?" Jamie pleads.

"Cross my heart, now get up," Zach says as he playfully reaches to tickle her mid-section.

While Jamie gets dressed Zach tells her he is going to the motel's office to get some coffee from the vending machine in the lobby.

She grabs Zach by the arm pulling him tight against her body, pleading with him not to leave without her.

"I'm afraid the men from the restaurant are outside the motel waiting for just this sort of opportunity to take you from me or worse they could decide they do not need you anymore and kill you," she pleads with tears forming in her eyes.

Zach reassures her with a gentle kiss to the forehead and a soft pat on the behind he says, "after we drove around half the night and then came all the way back to Dallas, picked a motel at random and stayed the entire night without a single incident."

"They're probably still driving around Houston like two lost puppies," he says feeling more confident now than he has in the past three days.

He gently kisses her on the mouth secretly wishing he could disappear with her like in the musical Brigadoon. In the story the whole town vanishes from sight and every one hundred years reappears for one day only to vanish again as quickly as it came, to be swallowed up and never seen again. She released Zach from her death grip and lowered her head, tears running down her face as he turned and stepped out the door into the still night shrouded morning.

First making sure that she locked the door behind him he turns and walks to the end of the second floor landing pulling the pistol from his boot when he reaches the top of the stairs. He descends the steps quietly, careful to make no sounds for even though he told her they were safe he knows that they had found him once back in Houston and they could find him again.

Seeing no one around the corner he starts down the long covered walkway—his shadow growing and shrinking under the glow of the overhead lamps as he passes under each one on his way to the motel's office. Getting to the office he looks around the motel parking lot for any suspicious goings on. Seeing none he stashes the pistol in his boot so the night manager does not see it and think he's robbing the place and walks into the lobby and over to the bank of vending machines. He starts plugging quarters into the machine that tiredly displays a picture of a coffee cup filled to the brim with supposedly 'Fresh Hot Colombian Coffee' as the banner states in big bold letters above the steaming cup.

Zach thought it odd that the night manager did not come out of the office when he walked into the lobby, and momentarily ceased feeding the machine quarters to look around the room for signs of a trap.

"He's probably in the bathroom," Zach says aloud, and hearing his voice echo in the small confines of the run down motel lobby suddenly sent a cold chill up his spine.

As if on cue, Zach hears a toilet flush to his right. Zach returns his gaze to the coffee cup that has just dropped down into the dispensing portion of the machine, and watches as the machine gives up its dark hot liquid from within. He is unaware of the large figure of a man stepping from the office and into the light of the lobby.

Chapter 16

July 22, 2000
4:40 a.m.
Star Bright Motel, Dallas, Texas

Whiteslayer has spent the entire night listening in to the room where Zach and Jamie made love, patiently biding his time. He is tired from the non-stop monitoring but he instantly shakes it off when he hears Zach wake Jamie and tell her that he is heading to the lobby of the motel to get them some coffee for their trip to the Airport. He gives Jake a hard shake to wake the snoring man.

"What?" Jake says startled out of a deep sleep.

"Get up. Now, damn it!" Whiteslayer adds impatiently as he gives the big man another hard shake for good measure.

Whiteslayer and Jake climb out of the van and quickly head around the corner and into the office. The night manager is dosing behind the check-in desk. His feet propped up on the counter, sitting in front of the TV that noisily displays a slow rolling snow pattern, the left over remains of a movie that ended almost two hours before, instantly followed by the station signing off the air.

The night manager jerks awake when he hears the two men come in and as quickly as his bent and twisted excuse for a body can move he stands and turns to greet the two new customers.

He is sure of two things as soon as the two men walk up to the counter. One, that they are not a couple of gay fellows looking for a place to spend an hour playing hide the salami, and two, this is about to be the worst day of his life.

"What can I do for you fellas," the night manager says as he slowly drops his right hand below the counter to where the 38 Special rests, waiting for just this sort of emergency.

Before he can reach the weapon, Whiteslayer whips out with his right hand and grabs the man by the neck, and drives his face into the counter. With a bone-crunching thud against wood the night manager lets out a loud wail. He manages to grab the gun with his right hand while reaching for his nose with his left, falling backward as the big man lets go of him. But he is only able to get the gun to mid-waist when he is shot between the eyes.

The night manager's body hits the floor with a thud as blood flows from the huge exit wound that is all that is left of the back of his head. With the silencer Whiteslayer has attached to the pistol, the rapport from the gun barely registers in the small lobby of the motel.

"Get him out of sight."

Quickly, Jake goes around the counter and drags the body though the door that leads into the small office that sits just off the lobby. Whiteslayer has already wiped up the blood from the counter where the night manager's nose connected with its smooth surface. He tosses the rags to Jake who bends and cleans the blood and bits of gray matter from the floor where the dead man fell.

After checking to see that everything was back in place, Whiteslayer stepped around the corner into the office motioning for Jake to take up a position in the men's room across the lobby.

After several minutes pass Zach finally enters the lobby and walks to the bank of machines along the same wall where Whiteslayer has taken position around the corner in the small office of the motel.

Whiteslayer steps out just has Zach picks up the freshly brewed cup of coffee and is about to deposit more coins into the machine to start a second cup of the dark addictive liquid brewing; oblivious to his stalkers sudden presence.

Whiteslayer steps out from the managers office pointing his Glock 9mm at Zach and says, "Well, hello, Zach."

Zach turns throwing the hot cup of coffee into Whiteslayer's face just as he is hit across the back of his head and is dropped by the butt of Jake's gun.

Chapter 17

July 22, 2000
4:55 a.m.
Star Bright Motel, Dallas, Texas

"Please come back," Jamie whispers softly through tears that are running down her cheeks while sitting on the edge of the bed trembling uncontrollably.

It has been fifteen minutes since Zach left for the motel lobby and he has not returned yet. She is starting to worry and the tears that she has fought to hold back have begun to flow as she waits. She gets up and paces across the floor, first to the small dresser and mirror that is pushed into one corner of the small room and then back to the bed where she momentarily sits back down.

She leaps to her feet and runs to the window when she hears the screeching tires of a van as it takes off out of the parking lot. She rushes to the window just as it turns onto the street and disappears out of sight. She starts for the door, her hand touching the dead bolt, but then hesitates for fear that they will be waiting for her just outside the door when she opens it.

Jamie goes back to the window to look out and see if anyone is outside. She cranes her neck to look first down one direction and then the other but sees nothing. Turning the gun over and over in her hands now, she sits by the window and waits hoping and praying she will see Zach come out of the office, but he never does.

Chapter 18

July 22, 2000
4:45 a.m.
Star Bright Motel, Dallas, Texas

Zach can feel himself sinking away into darkness, like a skipped stone that has lost its forward motion and slowly sinks beneath the cold black waters of a lake.

Zach is thrown into the back of the van; his hands bound behind his back as are his feet. He is oblivious of the rough handling by the two men as they climb into the van themselves and pull out of the motel parking lot.

Whiteslayer busies himself checking the burns that the hot coffee from Zach's cup has left on his face and neck while Jake throws the van into gear and pulls out of the parking lot with tires squealing.

"What about the girl?" Jake asks.

"We didn't come here for her." Whiteslayer says, "Zach is the only baggage I want to have to deal with on this return trip."

"What if she goes to the police? They're bound to ask questions."

"It doesn't matter since they will be looking for someone who no longer exists," Whiteslayer said with a grin.

"When Zach escaped from the compound we took precautions to make sure that all of his past records had been erased. And since his family is all deceased it will be hard to verify that he ever existed."

"When they can not find anyone by the name of Zach Denton living or dead who has ever worked for Technadine Corporation, they'll think she's lying and assume she had something to do with the killings at the restaurant."

"That should keep the cops busy and her out of our hair until operation 'Echo' is complete."

"By then we'll have the entire US government eating out of our hands and no one will be able to touch us."

Jake accelerates as he enters the highway that leads them out of Dallas and that will eventually take them and Zach back to Silicon Valley.

The combination of a mild concussion, thanks to the hard metal of Jake's pistol and three days of little or no sleep Zach has slipped deep into a dark and dreamless world where no one can enter and some have been known never to return.

Chapter 19

July 22, 2000
5:15 a.m.
Star Bright Motel, Dallas, Texas

Jamie slipped out the door of the motel room turning her head from one side to the other for the thousandth time to make sure that no one was waiting for her to exit the room. It had only been thirty minutes since Zach had left to go to the lobby of the motel to get them some coffee but it seemed like days to Jamie.

She cautiously moved down the walkway to the stairs pausing before each deserted room, afraid that as soon as she moved passed the doors a gruesome hand would reach out and wrap itself around her in a death grip pulling her kicking and screaming into the gloomy depths within.

Shaking off the thought she reached the stairs and peeked around the corner and down where the stairs moved along the wall of the motel and then made an abrupt one hundred and eighty-degree turn and ended at ground level facing the parking lot. Seeing that it was clear she hesitantly took the steps down one by one being as quiet as possible until she reached the bottom then stopped. Making sure there was no one behind her or in front, her spirits lifted as she caught sight of her car where her and Zach had left it the night before.

With a cry of relief Jamie ran to the car and unlocking the door she threw herself into the front seat instantly feeling the safety of its confines. Starting the engine she threw it into reverse and almost took the drivers side door off of it's hinges with one of the few remaining poles that held the awning in place before realizing she had left it partially open. She quickly shut it and backed out of the space and headed for the entrance to the motel and the safety of the street beyond.

She had almost made it to the street when she suddenly jammed on the brakes exclaiming to herself, "what if Zach is still in the lobby, hurt and unable to come out? What if he has been shot and left for dead? I can't just leave him there."

As much as she wanted to distance herself from the dreadful place she was equally drawn to the lobby to see if Zach was still in there. She pulled up to the front of the lobby entrance and reaching over and grabbing the pistol out of the glove box that she had taken from the man at the restaurant she climbed out of her car and stepped into the motel's lobby.

She immediately noticed the spilled coffee cup on the floor by the vending machine against the far wall, but otherwise the room was empty. The only sounds came from the television set that was currently showing one of those commercials featuring a plaque fighting mouthwash bottle complete with hands that seemed to float separate from it's body, wielding a sword and shield as it fought the evil plaque that invades teeth. The bottle was winning, she absently noticed.

She moved to the office door and peered into the room and jumped back with a start, just stopping the scream that welled up within her, when her eyes caught sight of the manager's body lying face up in a death stare.

"Oh my God!" she said as she quickly turned away from the horrible sight while fighting to hold back the bile rising up her throat.

She leaned heavily on the counter for several long seconds until the feeling began to diminish and she was once again able to catch her breath. She looked around the rest of the room and seeing that Zach was not in it she moved back into the lobby and towards the women's bathroom and peered inside. Seeing that it was empty she walked over to the door marked men's and pushed it open. A shadow darted in front of her with such speed she let out a scream and before realizing what she was doing raised the pistol she held in her hands shooting at the scurrying object.

The bullet careened off the floor ten feet away and plunged into the far wall tearing a large hole into the stucco wall. The noise from the gun caused several large rats to bolt from their current hiding places and scatter in all directions seeking new places to hide. With a scream, Jamie ran from the room and back through the lobby and out into the early morning light.

She did not stop shaking until she was almost to the freeway that headed back to Houston. With tears streaming from her eyes and afraid she would never see Zach again, she wondered if she could go on without him. Could she really return to her old job as if nothing had happened—just continue on with life as if he had never existed?

"No way in hell!" she exclaimed to herself.

She knew one thing for sure. Zach was still alive. They would not have killed him and then taken his body with them. As long as she believed that then she had the will to go on. She decided then and there she would go to the police and tell them everything that happened. Once she told the police her story they would be all over Technadine's headquarters. They would get Zach out and then she and Zach could go away together. She'd never have to be alone again. Jamie just knew that Zach was still alive and that she would see him again. How, or when she did not know. But she was determined not to give up hope. She dried her eyes and pulled out into the early morning traffic of downtown Dallas and headed back to an uncertain, but hopeful, future.

Chapter 20

July 22, 2000
11:00 am
Just west of San Antonio

Zach felt thick with sleep. His head throbbed from an angry headache. He was momentarily confused as to just where he was. Suddenly thinking that he and Jamie had slept too late and would miss the plane he tried to sit up and realized then where he was. Handcuffed and thrown in the back of a stripped cargo van he could just make out the two men sitting in the front seats their heads turned to the road ahead not paying any attention to him.

He struggled with the handcuffs trying to work his hand through the metal claw that gripped each wrist as tight as if he had been caught in a bear trap. The handcuffs were clamped so tightly around his wrist that his fingertips throbbed and tingled from the lack of blood flow. He also suddenly realized that his whole right arm tingled and ached from having lain on it for what Zach could only guess to have been at least a couple of hours. Zach was trying to turn his body so he could get some feeling back into his tingling right arm when Whiteslayer spoke.

"Well, look who has come back to the land of the living." Whiteslayer said as a devilish grin etched its way across his hard face.

Whiteslayer stood and moved to the back of the van where Zach lay, his massive body towering over Zach he said, "I trust you had a pleasant nap, I would not want to get a bad review from our esteemed scientist."

"It would be nice if you could loosen these cuffs on my wrist, I think they are cutting off the circulation in my hands," Zach said.

"Did you hear that, Jake? Our scientist friend here says his arms hurt," Whiteslayer said as he reared back and kicked Zach in the stomach.

"Now, maybe that will help you forget about the pain in your arms for awhile," he said as Zach curled into a ball from the blow, barely fighting back the urge to vomit.

Whiteslayer bent down until he was face to face with Zach, so close Zach could smell the mans sour breath as it came out in short choppy waves.

"I can't wait to get you back to the compound, Zach. We are going to have so much fun with you once you have finished making the other chips functional again."

"Who says I'm going to cooperate, shit head," Zach said to the big man and instantly regretted it.

Whiteslayer reached down and grabbed Zach by his testicles and squeezed making Zach cry out and bringing tears to his eyes.

"You will do what I say, when I say it, or I'll tear you apart piece by painful piece," Whiteslayer said as he tightened his grip with each syllable he spoke.

Zach started to black out but came to with a sharp slap by the big mans hand to his face. "Don't go away on me. We were just getting acquainted," he said.

Before Zach could respond Jake spoke up from the drivers seat of the van while straining to look in the rear view mirror at what was happening behind him. "Hey man, maybe you should leave him be. We shouldn't mess him up too much or he will not be very useful to us back at the compound."

"Hey, maybe you should go fuck yourself," Whiteslayer said to Jake who quickly shrunk back in the seat.

"Or maybe you'd like for me to take him back by myself," Whiteslayer said glaring at Jake.

"I didn't mean anything by it man. I'm sorry. Just forget it, OK?" Jake said.

"Just shut up and drive."

And then turned and with a wink to Zach said, "sleep tight," and hit Zach once with a quick jab to the jaw sending Zach again into darkness.

Chapter 21

July 22, 2000
11:30 p.m.
Somewhere in New Mexico

Zach heard Whiteslayer tell Jake to pull off the road so he could take a leak. Zach did not know how long it had been since he had come to after Whiteslayer had cold-cocked him but he knew by the darkness beyond the windows of the van that it was night out. The ride was a long one, especially when you are trussed up like a pig about to be barbecued. Zach needed to piss something terrible but he was almost too afraid to ask them if he could. The urge finally won out and he looked over at Whiteslayer and said, "you think I can take a leak too?"

Whiteslayer did not say anything at first but then turned to Jake and said, "you think I can trust you to keep an eye on him long enough so the man can piss?"

"Sure," is all Jake could manage to say. Then he added, "I think I can handle it."

"Like you handled it back at the restaurant?" Whiteslayer said with disdain.

Jake eased the van to the side of the road and threw it into park. He climbed out of the seat and went to where Zach was lying. He reached down and grabbed a handful of Zach's hair and yanked Zach into a sitting position and said, "don't try anything funny or I may have to let my buddy bounce his fist off of your face a few more times."

"I wouldn't think of it," is all Zach could manage.

Jake removed the handcuffs from Zach's hands and half-carried, half-threw him out the door. Jake shoved him around to the side of the van and said, "get to it. We haven't got all day."

It felt good to get on his feet after the long ride through two states tied up and lying on the cold hard metal floor of the van. Zach tried to take as long has possible so he could think of his options but Whiteslayer wasn't having any of it.

"Hurry it up, butt fuck, I want to get back by tomorrow and if I have to drag you all the way there I'll do it," Whiteslayer said.

Zach wanted badly to tell Whiteslayer to go fuck himself but his mind was saying don't do anything that will set him off. He needed to keep a cool head and just maybe he could find a way to get out of this. He thought of Jamie then and wondered what she was doing and if she was thinking of him. Zach hoped that she was ok and not too frightened.

He wondered if she would go to the police. What would they think when she told them the story? Zach knew that whatever story she told them, that it would lead to dead ends when it got back to Technadine. Zach knew that Morganthau would have covered his tracks well and would no doubt cover up any trace of Zach having ever worked there and probably that he even existed.

Zach was just trying to think of a way that he could contact Jamie when he was slapped hard in the side of the head by Whiteslayer. "Get back in the van butt head," Whiteslayer cursed. "I told you we haven't got time for your stalling. Lets go."

Before Zach could turn and climb back into the van a car approached from the west. As the car came along side the van it slowed but did not stop.

"Get in the van quick" Jake said to Zach as he instantly recognized the New Mexico State Trooper markings on the side of the car that just passed them.

Jake climbed in after Zach and went immediately to the front climbing into the driver's seat and throwing the car into gear, just as Whiteslayer himself had climbed into the passenger side of the van and closed his door.

"Drive slow in case he's stopped up ahead," Whiteslayer said of the police car that had slowed to take a better look at this group of three men standing by their van on the side of the road.

"We don't want to give him any excuses to pull us over."

They crested the next hill and saw the police car sitting on the shoulder of the breakdown lane two hundred yards up the road. As the van passed the parked Police car the state trooper hit his lights and pulled in behind the van. Jake hesitated for just a second before turning on his blinker and pulling the van to the side of the road.

Whiteslayer grabbed his pistol and jacked a round into the chamber, then turned to Zach and said, "don't make a sound unless you want the cop to wind up dead."

The police car edged up behind the van and rolled to a stop. The state trooper climbed from his patrol car and slowly walked to the van, his right hand resting on the butt of his revolver.

All of a sudden the back door of the van burst open and Zach leaped from the van running toward the patrol car, screaming.

"They have guns, they have guns!" Zach screamed as he lunged for the side of the patrol car and ducked behind the right front wheel.

The state trooper instantly pulled his revolver and went into a firing stance. He yelled to the two passengers in the van to put up their hands and exit the vehicle.

"Driver of the vehicle, exit the van now with your hands in the air!" the state trooper repeated.

"Passenger, exit the van through the driver's side of the van with your hands in the air."

Jake slid from behind the wheel and started to exit the van when Whiteslayer said, "go slow I'm going to be right behind you. When I say duck, hit the ground hard unless you want a bullet in the back."

Jake exited the vehicle and stood by the door facing the state trooper, who has now cautiously moved closer to the van. As Jake cleared the van's driver's side door Whiteslayer edged out of the vehicle with his arms raised.

Zach had started to run but realized there was no place to hide out here in the flat desert like conditions and that Jake and Whiteslayer could eventually find him. He was also holding out hope that the state trooper could successfully arrest the two before either of the two big men could pull anything. He wasn't taking any bets.

"Driver of the vehicle, walk forward three steps and then lay face down on the ground spread eagle," the cop said as he momentarily dropped his aim to point in the direction of the ground.

It was the break Whiteslayer need has he retrieved the pistol from his waistband that had been concealed by Jake's big frame. The cop had mistakenly moved too close to see immediately behind the big man and it left the perfect place to conceal a weapon as Whiteslayer now raised it and pulled off first one shot then a second. The first shot hit the state trooper, square in the chest knocking him backward. Not seriously hurt because of the bullet-proof vest he now regularly wore, the state trooper raised his own weapon as he fell to the ground from the force of the impact alone and managed to get off two shots of his own.

Whiteslayer leaped to his left as the first shot went high and to the right of his head. The second shot caught him high on the forearm taking out a chunk of meat from his left arm. Whiteslayer hit the ground hard and rolled over into a prone firing stance and lined up the barrel and squeezed off a shot just as the cop was starting to swing his own revolver in the direction that Whiteslayer had fallen. With cold indifference Whiteslayer said, "bye, bye", as he pulled off another shot striking the cop in the forehead just above his left eye. Skin and white bone flew from the wound as the cop fell backwards, dead before he hit the ground.

*   *   *

Jamie had made it back to Houston by 10:00 am and pulled into the restaurant parking lot to find the doors of the restaurant padlocked from the outside and crime-scene tape fluttering in the oven-like July wind. She had no idea what she was going to do and wondered if going to the police would even be helpful. She knew the whole story sounded like something out of a James Bond movie but she didn't know what else to do. Crying softly to herself she climbed back into her car and pulled out into the already busy traffic and headed to the nearest police station.

*   *   *

Whiteslayer stood and surveyed the damage. The good thing was no other cars had gone past them since the shooting had begun. But it wouldn't be long before someone came along and spotted the carnage.

"Jake! Get that little weasel back in the van and handcuffed and then help me get rid of the body." Whiteslayer fumed.

Jake went around to the side of the car where Zach had hidden and grabbed Zach by the shirt and half threw him toward the van. Before he could climb in Whiteslayer walked up to him and grabbed him around the throat and said, "this is your fault. If you didn't go trying to run none of this would have happened."

"I ought to kill you right now!" Whiteslayer screamed, frustrated that he couldn't carry out his own threat.

Instead, he threw Zach into the van and told Jake to hurry up with getting him handcuffed and turned his attention to dragging the cop's body from the road. He managed to get the body to the side of the road and into a sitting position against the left front tire of the police car. Whiteslayer retrieved the keys from the ignition and with Jake's help they easily picked up the body and carried it around to the trunk where they opened the trunk and tossed the body inside. Whiteslayer then instructed Jake to get in the vehicle and turn it toward the flat desert beyond the road. Tying off the steering wheel so it could not turn, Whiteslayer then wedged the cop's nightstick against the gas pedal and shut the car door. Finally he reached into the car and threw the gearshift into low drive and the car shot off on a slow roll into the desert night.

Whiteslayer climbed into the van and turned to look at Zach and said, "make no mistake Zach, one more trick like that and I'll forget all about bringing you back alive. That's your last and final warning."

*   *   *

Zach tried to sleep as they drove through the night but his mind would have none of it. Zach felt guilty for trying to escape back there in the desert. It was his fault that the state trooper was now dead. If he had only stayed quiet and not tried to escape and attract attention the policeman would probably still be alive.

He knew he was kidding himself. More than likely the cop had already deduced that something was wrong about these three individuals on the side of the road and was probably going to do a careful search of the van. He was as good as dead as soon as he decided to pull them over. The cop couldn't have known the kind of people he was dealing with.

"Such a waste," Zach thought.

He turned his thoughts to Jamie. If only there was some way he could get a message to Jamie then maybe, just maybe, there was a chance he could stop this. And just maybe he could escape with his life. Although he knew the chances of him getting out of this with his life was getting slimmer and slimmer. And the incident with the state trooper all but sealed his fate. They would never let him go, knowing he was now a witness to the capital murder of a policeman. But still, he held out hope. It was after all, all he had left. Zach finally did fall asleep but his sleep was restless and troubled, and of a girl with beautiful eyes the color of jade.

$$* \qquad * \qquad *$$

Jamie walked into the Houston Police department and for a moment thought of turning and walking back out, but before she could a heavyset policeman spoke up and asked her what she needed.

With a tremble in her voice she mentioned The Stables Eatery and everyone stopped speaking at once in the station house.

Jamie told them everything, or at least everything she could remember. From the moment Zach walked into the restaurant to when she got to the police station. Except for the amazing sex, which she decided was something no one needed to know about. She told them of the shoot out and how she ran to her car and started to flee but something made her stop and wait. She explained how Zach ended up in her car and how the two of them drove to Dallas and stayed the night in an old run down motel only to have Zach snatched away from her that morning.

The police station was buzzing and everyone was trying to make contact with investigators who had returned to the scene and were going over the evidence and reconstructing the events of the crime scene and were on the phone to Technadine trying to get some answers from them.

As Zach had feared, no records of his employment with Technadine existed and no one had ever heard of a man called Whiteslayer either. Jamie tried as best she could to explain the events and recall what was written in the pages of text that Zach had shown her but she was tired and upset and in the end all she could do was cry.

The investigators begin to think that this Zach character was more than he claimed to be and had maybe seen the chance to hook up with this young and quite attractive lady. They started to surmise that it was probably a drug deal gone badly and began to shoot holes in Jamie's story. After hours of going over the details again and again, Jamie had had enough. She was tired and scared and had begun to realize that they didn't believe her story. She felt she was wasting valuable time by being there and asked if she might be able to go home soon. Having exhausted all their questions and come up with zero answers and a lot of dead ends they agreed to let her go on the condition that she check in with them in the morning.

Jamie got back to her small apartment in the museum district of downtown Houston and collapsed on the couch and wept. She didn't know what she was going to do or even if there was anything she could do. She was tired and hungry, she knew that much, so she got up to get herself a soft drink and grabbed a handful of chips from the bag of store brand potato chips sitting on the kitchen table and headed for the bedroom.

She was about to head into the bathroom to take a shower when she suddenly had an idea. The police had immediately ask for the personnel department when they had called Technadine's headquarters but maybe if she could get connected to one of the outlying lab buildings, maybe they wouldn't have gotten the message that Zach was never there. She leaped over the bed and grabbed the phone off the hook and dialed information.

"The number for Technadine in California please," she told the operator.

A few seconds later a computer voice repeated the numbers and Jamie hurriedly wrote them down on a pad she kept by the bed.

Saying a quick prayer to herself she dialed the number to Technadine. After a couple of rings a sweet-sounding lady answered the phone.

"Excuse me, I have a shipment for one of the labs there at Technadine but the shipping receipt is hard to read and I was wondering if you can tell me what the name of your lab is?"

"Well, there are three labs here at Technadine, the Design lab, the Processor lab and the weapons lab," the operator replied.

"Oh, well it must be the Design lab that this shipment goes to. Could I trouble you to connect me with someone in that lab so that I can get some further information."

"Sure," said the operator, "please hold."

"Hi this is Chuck", said the voice that answered the phone. "Can I help you?"

"Yes, I was wondering if you could connect me with Zach Denton's office, please," Jamie asked.

"Sure, but I have to warn you he's not in today. I was just over there myself but did not see hide nor hair of him," Chuck said.

"Well, if it's alright I would like to leave a message on his voice mail"

"Sure lady, hang on and I'll patch you through."

"Before you go could you tell me his direct line?"

Chuck gave her Zach's number and then put her on hold while he transferred the call to Zach's voice mail. Jamie could not believe her luck. This was just the thing she was hoping for. Now if he just gets the message maybe she can help him to escape. Zach's voice mail came on and instructed the caller to leave a message after the tone.

"Zach, it's me. If you get this message call me at my apartment." Jamie left her phone number and then reluctantly hung up the phone. She was afraid that would be the last time she would get to talk to Zach and it made her well up with tears. "Please Zach, be alright."

Jamie had arrived at the police station around 10:45 am and been there for almost ten hours. It was now just 8:45 p.m. but Jamie felt like it was much later than it was. She was exhausted but she did not think she would be able to sleep even though she knew it was just what she needed. She threw back the blanket of the bed and grabbed her favorite teddy bear she kept by the pillow of her bed and laid down to try to sleep. Curling under the soft warm blanket and holding tight to "Ozzie", the name she gave to her favorite stuffed teddy bear, she thought of Zach and of their chances of ever seeing each other again.

She hoped and prayed that she would see Zach again and that he would be safe. She did not know if it was love she felt for him or not but she hoped she would get the chance to find out. She wanted to know more about Zach and what he was like. She wanted to hold him again and feel his arms wrapped tightly around her keeping her safe. Not five minutes after laying her head on the pillow she had fallen fast asleep thinking of Zach and holding tight to her stuffed teddy bear.

Chapter 22

July 23, 2000
6:00 am
Nevada, just outside of Las Vegas

Zach was roused from sleep with a soft kick in the stomach. Jake was standing over him and telling him to get a move on. Zach tried to get up but had trouble at first. Jake grabbed Zach by the shoulder and yanked him to his feet. "Come on I don't have all day."

Zach shuffled out of the van into the hot parched day that complimented the Nevada landscape. He was sure it was Nevada by the flat endlessly barren landscape that was totally void of trees. In the distance he could just make out a mountain range and knew that they weren't far from Red Rock Canyon. That meant that they would be in California in another six hours and he'd be face-to-face with Morganthau. He did not relish the thought one bit but knew it was just a matter of time.

They allowed Zach to use the restroom at the truck stop they had pulled into and had even bought him something to eat, which they casually tossed to him. "Here, this is for you. Do anything funny and it will be your last meal," Jake said.

Zach tore into the sandwich and drank half of the Coke before he decided he had better slow down. It wasn't the best sandwich he had ever eaten but he was not about to complain. The Coke was really what he needed and it took all his will power to not drink the entire thing in one mad gulp.

He could not remember the last time he had eaten. Then he remembered the restaurant and all the bloodshed and lost a bit of his hunger.

He started to think of trying to run but had finally decided it was useless to attempt. He knew that Whiteslayer would be able to catch him and he was not entirely sure if he would remain alive after that. He had made this a bad trip for them by knocking off two of their own before finally getting caught at the motel. He knew he was on thin ice with Whiteslayer and just about anything could set him off. Zach decided to wait and see if he could plan an escape once he got back to the compound.

He was painfully aware that it would be his only chance.

       *   *   *

Jamie stirred in her bed. The bed covers were a mess as if she had tossed and turned quite a bit in the night and she had slept in the clothes she was wearing when all this started. As she climbed out of bed to go pee she realized how sore and tired her whole body felt. It was as if she had been beaten with a baseball bat over her entire body.

She limped to the bathroom and took off her clothes and sat on the toilet to pee. When she had finished she went to the sink and turned on the water, turning the faucet up as hot has she could stand it. She washed her hands and then cupped her hands under the flow of the now steaming water and brought it to her face. Even though it was practically scalding it felt good to her skin. She grabbed a towel from the linen closet and walked to the shower and turned it on. Not waiting for the temperature to adjust she climbed into the shower and let the water cascade over her aching shoulders and down her back.

"It feels good to be home and in my own shower," she thought has she let the water run over her entire body. The stinging spray made her nipples hurt as the water pulsated over her skin but she didn't care. It felt so good to be alive.

Then she thought of Zach and how good it felt to make love to him. How wonderfully fulfilling the experience had been. Thinking of the sex had begun to arouse her and she found herself moving her hand over her swollen nipples and then slowly down to the thatch of hair between her legs.

The feeling rekindled the whole night with Zach and she wanted so much to feel the moment again but she knew she would just be teasing herself and no amount of touching could bring back the way it felt with Zach. Jamie grabbed the bottle of shampoo with a sigh and started washing her hair. When she had finished and had begun to dry off she was hit with an idea.

"Hey! What if I pretend I'm delivering a package to the lab? That way I could sneak in and help Zach to escape!" she said as she stared at her tired reflection in the mirror above the sink. Almost immediately she had began to have second thoughts.

"I'm no Superwoman or even Batman and Robin, how am I going to get him out of there? They will probably have him chained to his desk or at the very least locked in a room that I would not be able to gain access to. I have got to come up with something but, in the meantime, I know one thing I've got to do and that's go there. If I'm going to be able to help Zach it is going to have to be in California."

Chapter 23

July 23, 2000
11:30 am
Silicon Valley, California

Zach knew that they were getting close to the office. He was pretty sure that four or five hours had passed since they had stopped in Nevada. A little more than half an hour later his intuition paid off as Jake spoke up for the first time since the Truck Stop. "Well, home sweet home."

Whiteslayer said, "take the service entrance and go over behind the design lab and pull up next to the last bay door."

"Roger that," Jake said.

"We'll get him secured in his lab and get Rusty posted outside the door and then we will go up and see Morganthau."

"Man, do I have to go with you? I am not at all looking forward to a chat with him." Jake said.

"You will do what I say and like it," Whiteslayer snapped.

They pulled up next to the large bay door and checking to make sure no one else was around went around to the back of the van and opened the door.

"Get out, now," Whiteslayer said.

"I'm coming boss," said Zach.

They both grabbed Zach's arms, one on each side of him, and marched him up the stairs and through the door leading into the

Technadine Design Labs Receiving office. The usual workers were out on runs and the office was empty except for Whiteslayer, Jake and Zach. They took him down the hall and through the security check where Rusty was sitting and eating a sandwich.

Rusty was surprised to see Whiteslayer and Jake back so soon and was about to ask them about the trip but Whiteslayer spoke up first.

"Get off your ass and let us through. We don't have all day here." And then added, "since when do we eat on the job?" Whiteslayer growled.

"Sorry," is all Rusty could say.

Whiteslayer half-carried, half-dragged Zach to Zach's office. Opening the door Whiteslayer then shoved Zach into the room hard enough to cause Zach to collide with one of the lab tables.

"Stay put," is all Whiteslayer said has he shut and locked the door that was the only way in or out of the big lab.

Whiteslayer walked back to the security station and told Rusty not to let anyone in or out of the building, period.

"Gotcha," Rusty replied.

Rusty was already tired of this gig. He had hired on just two months earlier and he already didn't like the tight security and the way Whiteslayer treated him but he was not about to tell him to his face. The man was dangerous and had a short fuse to boot. He tried his best to give the Indian a wide berth.

Jake on the other hand wasn't a half-bad guy and he would often talk with the big man about soldiering and stuff. They seemed to hit it off and had quite a bit in common. Both he and Jake were into deer and elk hunting and they both shared an interest in taxidermy. They would often regale each other about their hunting exploits each trying to out do the other.

But Rusty had grown weary of the place soon after coming to work there, especially when this business with Denton, the lab technician had begun. He quickly realized that these guys played hardball. They did not just make the rules; they went out of their way to beat them into you.

Rusty always considered himself a tough character especially since he weighed in at 255 pounds and stood six feet three inches tall. He had played college football for Notre Dame and won several accolades for his on-the-field exploits. He had joined the Marines after college spending four years touring the World's hotspots with the UN peacekeeping forces. He had grown tired of that gig too.

It was not that he didn't like the Marines, it just kept him away from his girl, Amanda. Rusty was as tough as they come but when it came to girls he went 'all soft' in the middle. He liked being with Amanda and after he got out of the service he married her and they moved to Silicon Valley where she got a job working for a lab that makes microchips. He did not have too many skills that came in handy in this neck of the woods except the security gig, so he hired on at Technadine and made the best of it until something better came along. He had been thinking of going back to school to become a real estate agent because he could see by the size of the houses in the valley that real estate agents probably made a killing in commissions.

He was hoping to start back to school this coming fall and maybe start looking for a local real estate company to hire on with by the following year. Until then, he would just have to stick it out at Technadine and try not to piss off Whiteslayer or anyone else for that matter.

Rusty was just contemplating his future when Morganthau, Whiteslayer and Jake entered the building and approached his desk.

"Well, lets have a look at our fugitive shall we, Rusty," Morganthau said.

Rusty jumped up and snatched the keys from his belt and went over to the door that led into the labs where Zach was now confined. He quickly unlocked the door and stepped aside so Morganthau could open the door.

"Well, it is good to see you Zach," said Morganthau sarcastically as he opened the door to the lab and stepped inside.

"You and your little girlfriend have caused me quite a lot of grief Zach. But just so you know, the Houston and Silicon Valley police have run into a lot of dead ends when it comes to your identity. And, thanks to that little bitch friend of yours they now think it was a drug deal gone sour at the restaurant so they have effectively ceased investigations here at Technadine. So you can rest assured you will be left alone to complete the remaining chips."

"So, now that we have your undivided attention I expect the remaining chips to be complete by the end of the week and then I guess you'll be allowed to go."

"Come on now, you and I both know you have no intention of letting me go. I'm as good as dead when those chips are finished," Zach said.

"If you think I'm going to make those chips functional so you can deploy your little scheme you can think again."

Morganthau gave Whiteslayer a slight nod and in a flash Whiteslayer reached out and punched Zach in the ribs hard enough to hear an audible "crack" as Zach doubled over and slumped to the floor in pain. Before he could recover Whiteslayer had grabbed him by the hair and yanked him off the ground and taking one of his arms had twisted it around behind him. For good measure Whiteslayer bent Zach's wrist until a noticeable "pop" was heard in the room. Zach let out a scream of pain and fell again to the floor now holding his broken wrist gingerly in his other hand.

Morganthau silently and with a slight smile splayed across his lips watched as Whiteslayer swiftly dealt out his punishment. With a wave of his hand, Morganthau stopped the attack and said, "Zach I do hope you understand that you will do what we ask or I will be forced to have Whiteslayer here dish out a little more of his enthusiasm."

"All right, all right, you win," said Zach through clenched teeth. The pain in his side was making it hard to speak. "I'll do what ever you want. But with my hand broken I'm going to need some help with the work."

"Fine," said Morganthau. "Rusty here can help you when you need it. Right Rusty?"

"Uh, sure," Rusty said from the doorway, not really wanting to be any part of this.

"Good, so we are all in agreement then," Morganthau said as he walked to the door.

Just before he walked away for good Morganthau turned and said, "remember Zach, I want all of the chips operational by the end of the week. That means you have 48 hours to get them done. Get them done and I will think about letting you live."

Morganthau stepped through the door past Rusty and was gone. Whiteslayer turned to Rusty and said, "make sure he gets what ever he needs to complete the job," and then walked out after Morganthau.

Jake, not knowing what to do decided he had had enough of this for one day and headed off to his office in the main building. He decided there was a bottle of Jack Daniel's with his name on it waiting in the bottom drawer of his desk and he did not want to waste any more time getting to it.

Zach was left alone in the room with Rusty standing just outside the open doorway. Before shutting and locking the door Rusty said, "Let me know when you need me and I'll come on down."

"Thanks, I can't wait," Zach could barely manage.

When Zach was finally left alone he limped over to his office and sat behind his small desk in the corner of the room. The office was a small room in the corner of the lab. It was just large enough to hold a desk and a file cabinet and a couple of chairs. It wasn't much but then he rarely spent any time in here if at all. All of his time was devoted to the lab and his work so he never really needed the office to begin with. It had been Morganthau's idea to have the office in the lab so it would be close to his work.

"Such a nice guy that Morganthau," Zach thought.

He sat down behind his desk and was about to push his way over to the file cabinet when he noticed the blinking light on his phone indicating that he had several messages. He stared at the light and at first thought about not checking the messages. He knew they would be from vendors and from other lab technicians within Technadine wanting to chat with him about one thing or another. He had almost talked himself out of listening to them when he thought of Jamie and wondered if just maybe she had been able to get in touch with him. He reached over and pushed the button and sat back favoring his right wrist as the messages began to play.

*   *   *

Jamie waited and waited for the phone to ring hoping that Zach somehow had gotten her message and would soon call. She knew it was a long shot to expect him to receive the message knowing that Morganthau would probably deny him access to a phone but it was their only chance and so she sat by the phone hoping and praying for a miracle.

Jamie was about to get up and get herself something to drink when the phone rang. She clasped her hand to her chest with a start and then reached for the phone.

"Miss Fry," the voice said.

"Yes."

"This is Detective Thomas with the Houston Police department. Do you have a few seconds to talk?"

Jamie blew a sigh of relief and slight disappointment as she relaxed her hold on the phone.

"Yes detective what can I do for you," not really wanting to talk but knowing she would have to anyway.

*   *   *

Zach listened to the messages as they rolled off the recorder hitting the delete button as each one finished replaying. There were quite a few of them and he was quickly getting bored with them and thought of stopping when he heard Jamie's voice.

Zach did not waste time punching in the number that Jamie left on his machine. His first attempt produced a busy signal, which he took as a good sign.

"At least she is home," Zach said to the empty room.

He tried the number again a few minuets later and with a sigh of relief heard the phone ring on the other end.

"Hello?" came Jamie's tired voice through the receiver.

"Jamie!" Zach yelled nearly falling out of his chair.

"Oh Zach! I'm so glad you got through. Are you all right?"

"Yea, I'm fine Jamie. Just some bumps and bruises but I will live…for now," he added.

"I have been worried sick that they had killed you and I would never get to see you again," she replied as tears started to form around her eyes.

"I'm fine babe. But I need your help getting out of here," Zach said.

"What can I do? I went to the police Zach, but I do not think they believed me. They made comments like they thought it was some kind of drug deal gone sour. They even contacted someone at Technadine but officials there denied having anyone by your name working for them."

"I figured as much Jamie. I knew that Morganthau would have covered up my ever having worked for him. In fact he has probably erased my entire identity by now so there is no trace that I ever existed."

"Can he do that?" Jamie asked.

"In the position he is in he can do almost anything he wants and the government will turn a blind eye."

"So what can we do?"

"Well for starters I need you to fly to California. Can you get a flight out today?"

"I'll try," Jamie said.

"I have been given 48 hours to complete the chips and get them ready for transfer so whatever we do has to be done by tomorrow at the latest."

"What happens if you don't do what they ordered?" Jamie asked.

"Well, I'd say that I'm a dead man, Jamie."

"Oh please don't think that Zach. Maybe they will let you go when you finish the chips."

"I doubt it Jamie. I have seen the look in Morganthau's eyes. I don't think he has any intention of letting me go alive."

"Jamie we need a plan, a diversion of some kind. Something that will distract everyone in the buildings and knock them off guard just long enough to give me a chance to escape. Then if I can get past the guard here in the lab I could meet you outside of the design lab and we could drive straight to the airport and get a flight south. Somewhere preferably far away from these bastards."

"But how will you get past the guard?" Jamie asked.

"That's a good question. I will just have to think of something. In the meantime I need you to get up here as soon as possible. I do not know how long I will have a phone so we need to plan it now in case we are cut off from each other later."

Jamie thought for a second and then said, "what if I started a fire in the main building somewhere. Wouldn't they have to evacuate the building?"

"That's it!" Zach exclaimed.

"And here is how you're going to do it."

Zach filled her in on the items she would need to start a fire and where she should start it. They went over just what time they should start the diversion and settled on where Jamie should be when Zach makes his break.

"Now remember get out of the building as fast as you can and drive around to the first lab building behind the main office tower. Pull around back and to the nearest bay door at the back of the building. I will come out of the small door next to that bay door."

"But how will you get by the guard?" Jamie asked.

"I don't know yet but I will think of something. In the meantime get here as quick as you can and be ready."

"I will Zach." Jamie cried.

"Don't cry Jamie." Zach said. "Everything will be all right. I promise."

"I hope your right Zach," she cried.

"I hope your right."

Chapter 24

July 23, 2000
1:30 p.m.
Museum District, Houston Texas

Jamie grabbed a change of clothes from her closet and threw them into her overnight bag. She ran into the bathroom and came out a few seconds later carrying an armload of bathroom necessities. She stuffed them into her bag as well. After a brief look around the room, went to her night stand and took the picture of her dad that she kept by her bed and held it up to her face; planted a kiss on the picture and said, "dad I love you. Wherever you are."

She laid the picture on top of the other items in her overnight bag and then zipped the bag shut. She was not sure she would be able to come home again and for a moment she just stood where she was, tears softly rolling down her cheek.

She thought back on all the things her dad had taught her and of the good times that they had had when she was a little girl. She was thinking of the days her and her dad would sit on the porch swing watching the horses in the field and talking about the future. Her dad had wanted her to go to college and had dreams of his little girl one-day being married and having children of her own. He always told her to follow her heart and it would never lead her astray.

"I hope you are right dad. My heart says to help Zach and make a life with him no matter where we end up. I think he's the one dad. I know we will be happy together. I just know it. I think my heart does too."

Jamie grabbed the overnight bag off the bed and headed out of the apartment. She stopped in the kitchen and left a note for the manager of the apartment complex with instructions to sell off the remaining items in the apartment and to use the money to pay off the rent she still owed. She told him that she hoped it would be enough. She left the note by the refrigerator and headed for the door grabbing her keys off the table as she went. She stopped one last time and turned and looked at her life that she was leaving behind, wondering what kind of life Zach and her would share and if it would last. She hoped it would. She prayed it would last a lifetime.

*   *   *

Zach busied himself making the last adjustments to the microchips that remained and trying to think up a plan to disable the guard so he could make his escape. He had no idea how or what he could do to get pass Rusty but he also didn't want to harm the guy either. He could tell that Rusty was not like the rest of the security team that Morganthau had at his beck and call. Rusty had a good heart about him and so Zach sat and thought about what he could do that would disable Rusty but not hurt him in any way.

He was just forming a plan in his mind when he heard someone at the door. Whiteslayer strolled into the room and without saying a word walked straight for Zach's office. A crash was heard and then Whiteslayer came walking out holding the phone in his big beefy hands.

"Just so you don't get any ideas," Whiteslayer said. "We wouldn't want you calling your mommy."

"Damn," Zach said sarcastically, "and I was going to order us all a pizza."

Whiteslayer started toward Zach with a glint of hate in his eyes but stopped and deciding it was not worth the time or trouble, turned and headed for the door. He stopped at the door, turned and said, "you will do wise to watch the smart mouth, Zach. Or maybe you would like for me to break the other wrist too?"

Zach said nothing. He just stared at Whiteslayer knowing that someday the tables would turn on him and he would get what was coming to him.

Whiteslayer turned and with a smug look on his face stormed out of the room, closing and locking the door behind him.

Zach sat there staring at the door not sure what to do. He would not be able to contact Jamie now that was for sure. He just hoped against hope that their plan went off without a hitch and he could escape from the lab, that is, if he could think of a way to disable the guard.

*   *   *

Jamie's plane left the Houston heat and sunshine at just after 4:00 p.m. and banked sharply to the West Northwest and began it's slow climb into the clouds. After stabilizing at 30 thousand feet, according to the pilot, the stewardesses began their customary rounds of taking drink orders but when they got to Jamie she just shook her head that she wanted nothing and turned to stare out the tiny window by her seat in 41B. She had lots of time to think about her and Zach's plan and the last thing she needed was to get drunk.

She once again thought of her dad and under her breathe said, "I hope you're looking out for your little girl this time daddy, cause I am sure going to need all the help I can get."

*   *   *

Zach tried to think of some way he could lure Rusty into the room and disable the big man without hurting him. The sharp pain in his side every time he took a breath and the pain from his right hand made it difficult to think clearly. The only idea he could come up with was to temporarily blind him by spraying him with the fire extinguisher.

But he had to somehow get the big man to the lab table and away from the door so he could have a clear shot at the only exit in the room. He also hoped that Rusty would leave the door unlocked after he entered the room or he would have to wrestle the keys away from the big man somehow. He knew he would be no match against the size and obvious strength of someone as big as Rusty. All he could do was hope that things went the way he planned, if they did not, then he was sunk.

*   *   *

Jamie dozed off and on during the flight to California. She turned down the meal the stewardess had handed her but ask if she could bring her a soft drink instead. The soft drink was welcomed refreshment and it had the desired affect of waking her from her restless slumber. She went over the plan in her head for the thousandth time, trying to improve on it in some small way to ensure there would be no mistakes when the real deal started to happen. She was obviously nervous and scared for what might happen to Zach if things didn't work out like they had planned. She did not want to think about what might happen if they caught Zach trying to escape. She did not even think what might happen to her if they caught her. It never even entered her mind. That was how important it was to her to get Zach out of there. Nothing mattered but being with Zach again.

The flight touched down about 7:00 p.m. California time but Jamie waited for the other passengers to disembark before standing and retrieving her overnight bag from the storage compartment above her seat. Jamie walked to the front of the plane and strolled into the main terminal of the San Francisco International Airport. She had never been out of the state of Texas before and had no idea how to go about getting transportation so she could drive the two hours it would take to get to Silicon Valley. She stopped at one of the information booths in the main terminal building and asked for directions to the nearest rental car agency.

Walking down the long concourse reminded her of strolling through one of the many malls back home in Houston. Shops of every kind lined the walkway and she was taken aback at the shear number of people the place could handle.

"You could put the whole town of Alvin in this place and still have room left over for all the shops you could ever dream of having," she thought.

The shear size of the place made Jamie feel like a lost little girl in a big crowd. She never imaged places like this existed. She knew Houston was a big place and often felt out of place in the big city but this was almost too much to handle. She was practically being herded along by the mass of people that moved like one big frantic wave and she almost missed the rental car counter as the crowd of busy travelers swept her along. She managed to work her way to the edge of the crowd of people and over to the counters that made up the check-in and checkout area for the Swift Rental Car Company.

She handed the clerk her driver's license, insurance card and her credit card and was asked to sign some papers and informed of some special offers, which she declined. After all of the paper work was in order she was handed the keys to a silver Mercury Sable and pointed in the direction of the courtesy van that would take her to the rental car lot on the outskirts of the huge airport.

After the long drive to the car lot and the equally long walk to the assigned rental car she climbed behind the wheel and fussed with the controls to make herself comfortable. Once everything was in order and she felt at ease behind the wheel of the unfamiliar car she began going over the map the clerk at the rental counter had given her showing her the way to Silicon Valley.

The clerk had said that Silicon Valley was a short drive due South along Hwy 101. She had said that you couldn't miss it because it looks like you just arrived in a glass city because all of the buildings were surrounded in glass and the whole place shimmered in the morning light.

Jamie decided after the long plane ride and the fact that she hadn't eaten on the plane, to stop at the first place she saw and get something to eat. She wanted to make good time and get settled in a room before it got too late but she thought she could handle the drive better on a full stomach. She pulled into the first fast food place she came to which happened to be a McDonalds and ordered a meal to go. She pulled out of the parking lot and turned South on Hwy 101 and headed toward Silicon Valley and an unknown future.

*   *   *

Zach sat on the stool and stared at the state-of-the-art equipment he used in the production of his microchips. The room adjoined the lab and was sealed by an air lock to prevent contamination of the room. He wanted nothing to do with the equipment now. He had lost his drive, his willpower. He wondered how he had become so consumed with the idea of artificial intelligence and what had drove him to take this job with Technadine in the first place.

He knew it was because he had been passionate about his life's work, his dream of creating the first true artificial intelligent system. A system that could reason and learn on it's own without human involvement. But he could not understand why his passion had driven him so. He had lost that passion now and he knew nothing would ever bring it back. He was also tired and knew that he should try to get some rest and heal his wounds as best he could. The morning would get here soon enough and he had better be ready if he hoped to escape with his life.

Zach slid slowly off the stool and walked to his office. He eased himself into his comfortable leather chair and tried to relax. He knew it was going to be a long night with nowhere to stretch out and sleep; the chair was his best bet. He had doused the lights of the office when he had entered and only the lab's lights were still on. If he had to get up in the middle of the night he did not want to run the risk of tripping over something and injuring him self any further than he already was.

As he sat there he thought of Jamie and those beautiful jade green eyes and how much he missed holding her in his arms. He prayed their plan would work, and he also prayed that the guard would be distracted long enough for him to slip out. He only hoped that Jamie could get here in time and provide the necessary distraction. His life was riding on whether or not things went according to plan. He did not want to think of the consequences if they did not.

Chapter 25

Jamie entered through the huge double glass doors that formed the entrance to Technadine Corporations first floor lobby. She stopped at the receptionist desk and waited while the secretary finished speaking on the phone.

"Can I help you?" the lady behind the desk inquired as she set down the receiver.

"Yes, I was wondering if you were currently accepting applications for employment?" Jamie replied.

"We are always looking for individuals to fill some new position management has dreamed up," the receptionist said.

"Let me get you an application form to fill out and you can sit right over there if you like and complete it right now or if you like you can take it with you and bring it back at your convenience," she said.

Jamie replied, "if it is all the same to you I'd just as soon fill it out now. With the way the job market is right now, the sooner I can get a chance to interview the better."

"I know what you mean," the lady behind the desk said, "I was out of work for two months before I finally got hired on here, just three weeks ago."

"Well, I hope it does not take me that long to get a response or I will be in bills up to my neck," Jamie told the receptionist.

The nice receptionist handed Jamie the necessary forms and pointed in the direction of the chairs that lined the wall of the foyer.

"Well I hope you get hired on, it would be nice to have someone new to go to lunch with besides all of these nerdy scientists around here," the nice lady said.

"With all of these serious types around here all the time, this place could use some livening up," the receptionist added.

"Well I would sure like to be the one who gets to do it," Jamie told her, and thinking to herself, if all goes as planned there should be some major livening up in this place about ten minutes from now.

Jamie turned and headed for the chairs by the wall and then stopped and turned back to the receptionist and said, "pardon, me but could you tell me where the restrooms are? I've been on my feet all morning and I really need to use the ladies room."

The receptionist behind the desk said, "sure," and pointed her in the direction of the hallway to Jamie's right saying, "just down the hall and the second door on the left."

"Thank you," Jamie replied.

Jamie turned and headed down the long tunnel-like hallway, hoping none of the men that had been chasing them would show up right now and spoil her chance to help Zach. She knew Zach was somewhere in the design lab and no doubt waiting for the signal he had communicated to her the night before. As she pushed open the door to the bathroom a familiar face rounded the corner from another doorway several doors down the hall and headed toward her direction. He seemed to take no heed of her as he strolled by except for a slight smile on his face. She slipped into the bathroom pushing the door closed behind her. Jamie leaned against the door trying to steady her obviously shaking body as she realized that the man she saw was the very same one that she had kneed in the groin back at the restaurant.

"Maybe he was lost in thought or just plain didn't recognize me," Jamie thought.

Before she left the hotel she had cut and dyed her hair black and changed her make-up in order to disguise her appearance just in case she ran into one of the men that had chased them. Knowing that she could not possibly pass herself off as a job applicant in blue jeans, Jamie had packed a change of clothes to give the appearance that she was a potential job applicant looking for work in a large corporation.

She was simply dressed in a white blouse and gray skirt with matching shoes. She had also purchased a large gray purse, which was big enough to contain the items that Zach had instructed her to bring with her.

Once inside the bathroom Jamie had to stop and try to compose her nervousness. She was scared to death that someone would come along and catch her starting the fire before she had the chance to escape and help Zach. When Jamie felt she had her trembling hands under control she quietly opened the door and peeked out as far as she dared to see if anyone was waiting to grab her when she came out. The hallway was empty and the building eerily quiet.

She closed the bathroom door and locked it from the inside. Checking each stall as she went down the line until she came to the last one on the right she opened the door and stepped inside. Laying the large bag she had earlier purchased at the store on top of the commode's tank, she removed the contents that Zach had instructed her to bring. She took out three large aerosol cans of hair spray, butane lighter, a bottle of charcoal lighter fluid and a tube of butyl rubber caulk.

Working quickly she climbed up on top of the commode and just barely reaching the ceiling tile she pushed one of the panels aside. Jamie opened the tube of caulk and squeezed out as much of the black goo as she could along the wall that divides the bathrooms leaving the tube at the end of the trail of rubber. She then took two of the cans of hair spray and laid them next to the bead of caulk.

Taking the bottle of charcoal lighter fluid Jamie began to soak the bead of caulk she had just laid down as well as the two cans of hair spray and the surrounding ceiling tile panels and several electrical cables that were nearby. When she had just about emptied the bottle of fluid, being careful to leave a small amount still in the bottle she capped it and then threw it has far as she could into the crawl space between the floors.

She removed the cap from the third can of hair spray being careful to point it into the crawl space. With her right hand she took out the butane lighter and struck the flint with her right thumb until a flame appeared, first with a bright flicker and then settling down to an orange-red glow. Jamie placed the flame in front of the nozzle of the spray can about eight inches away and slightly below the level of the nozzle.

"I hope this works," she said as she depressed the nozzle of the spray can releasing its contents.

For a brief second nothing seemed to happen, then with a rush of heat the crawl space in front and to both sides of her was consumed in thick flames. She continued to empty as much of the aerosol spray into the spreading fire as she could stand until the heat was too much, then tossed the remains of the can into the crawl space and jumped down from the stall. It had only been a few seconds since she struck the lighter but the whole room was already engulfed in a thick black smoke from the butyl rubber that was now bubbling from the intense heat.

Jamie had just made it to the door when one of the cans of aerosol spray exploded causing the flames to shoot out of the opening where she had been just seconds ago.

Jamie exited the ladies room and half-ran-half-walked to the entrance, stopping briefly at the receptionist counter and said, "if I were you I'd get the hell out of this place, and now!"

Before the nice receptionist can say a word the emergency alarm sounds and then the room is showered with water from the emergency water sprinklers. She looks up into the falling rain and back down at Jamie with a surprised look on her face but Jamie is already running toward the front doors to the building. The receptionist is momentarily confused and then instinctively she reaches for her umbrella as if she has suddenly found herself caught in a summer shower. The receptionist comes to her senses and drops the umbrella and runs for the door that Jamie had just exited seconds before.

Jamie raced to her car and jumped in. Starting the car she threw it into reverse and smashed down hard on the accelerator. The car flew out of the parking space crashing into a black Mercedes Benz parked in the slot just opposite the one she is parked in. She throws the lever into drive and stamps on the gas. With screeching tires, she speeds out of the parking lot and around the corner of the building to the side street where the design lab is located and pulls around the corner to where the entrance is located for deliveries. She almost reaches the spot where Zach has told her to wait when a man comes running out of the building just to her right.

At first, thinking it is Zach she almost stops the car, then realizes it is the man that she saw in the hallway just ten minutes ago and the one that she had kneed in the crotch back at the restaurant.

*   *   *

After returning to his office, Jake planted himself in the soft leather chair that came with the office Technadine had given him when he signed on to be Assistant Chief of Security. The title was beefy and the pay was good but the job was nothing more than hand holding, or at least it was until this situation with Zach came down on top of them. Now all of a sudden they're hip-deep in several murders, including the killing of a cop no less. He needed a stiff drink or two. The shit was really starting to fly around here and his nerves needed a quick shot to calm then down.

He had just reached into the drawer of the credenza that sat against one wall opposite his desk and removed a bottle of Jack Daniel's from behind a stack of papers when he suddenly realized where he had seen the girl before. She had been entering the restroom in the lobby when he came around the corner and it suddenly registered where he had seen her before. She was the same girl that he had grabbed at the restaurant and who had kneed him in the balls. The hair was different but he would never forget a body like that. Never in a million years could he forget the way that dress clung to every curve of her body.

"Son of a bitch," he said as he quickly picked up the phone and alerted Whiteslayer that she was here. Just has he got off the phone the fire alarm sounded and he knew that the girl was behind it.

"Shit!" Jake said as he grabbed his gun off of his desk and bolted for the door. He ran down the long hall and around the corner to the side door of the building just as someone walked out of an office, colliding with him in the hallway. The two of them went sprawling across the floor; papers the other person had been carrying went flying in all directions. Without apologizing Jake leaped to his feet and ran for the door.

He was almost to the parking lot between the main building and the lab where Zach was locked away when he heard a car speeding around the corner. Jake instantly knew that it was the girl from the restaurant and began running toward her as he reached for the gun tucked away in the shoulder holster inside his suit jacket. He ran out into the parking lot and just started to raise his pistol when the car changed directions and headed straight for him.

He tried in vain to leap out of the way of the speeding vehicle but was too late as it hit him at mid-waist sending him flying up onto the hood of the car. Jake's last thought was how bright the sunlight glinted off the chrome of the bumper and how it seemed to dance across the grille as if it were many brightly colored objects playfully moving over the car.

*   *   *

Jamie barely has time to think as she stamps down hard on the accelerator, launching the car at the man. Before he can react, the car's bumper connects with the man at mid-waist knocking his legs out from under him. His body is thrown on to the hood of the car hard enough to leave an impression of his face as well as a lot of blood on the hood of the car. Jamie hits the breaks and the lifeless body slowly slides off the cars hood and falls in a heap on the ground.

"Oh my God, I killed him," Jamie says as she begins to cry, and all the while frantically looking around and wondering where Zach is and why has he not shown up yet.

Chapter 26

July 24, 2000
9:00 a.m.
Design Lab, Technadine Laboratories

Zach sat in his lab still sore from the beating he'd received from Morganthau's men the night before. He was having trouble removing the fire extinguisher from the wall by the door. The weight of the bottle made him strain to hold on to it and it sent excruciating needles of pain coursing through his rib cage where Whiteslayer had punched him and broken a rib. He carried the bottle over to the lab's long stainless steel counter where various experiments were performed and set it down on the front side of the counter out of view from the doorway.

The exertion from carrying the bottle made it hard for him to breathe and he felt like he had just ran a marathon. The sharp pain in his left side where they had used him for a punching bag had increased overnight and he was stiff from sleeping in his office chair. His beating was their attempt to try and impress upon him the importance of finishing the project and unlocking the codes to the remaining Hal2001 chips.

What Morganthau and his henchmen did not know is that he had completed the task soon after arriving back at the lab. Zach had also made a few minor adjustments to the chips to insure that their future capabilities were, "how to put it, set to receive a ringing send off," Zach thought with a pain-laced smile. He had just completed the last chip and had placed it in it's case, and was now working on a much more desperate project, to try and escape before they came back and finished the job from last night.

He was planning to surprise the guard who was sitting by the door reading a soldier of fortune magazine and smoking a Camel cigarette.

"God, these guys were hopeless, even when there was no place to fight they sat around dreaming about it," Zach thought to himself.

Zach knew that he could not get by the guard in the condition he was in so he devised a plan to get the guard to come over to the lab table by telling him he needed help to complete the testing of the chips. He knew time was running out. Jamie was bound to have entered the building and was probably in the process of creating a diversion. Any second he expected to hear the alarms go off in the building and knew he would have to disable the guard before the proverbial shit hit the fan, otherwise the guard would get the upper hand and secure the room and seal Zach's fate.

*   *   *

Jamie was becoming more and more nervous as the seconds ticked away. She was watching the hundreds of people running, stumbling and being crushed under foot as they fled the fire she had started in the building moments earlier. She could already hear sirens as the fire stations were summoned by the automatic alarms and had dispatched the fire trucks to the scene. Jamie figured that she had maybe three minutes maximum before the place where she was now parked would be crawling with cops and firemen. She decided to get out of the car and see if she could move the body of the guy she had hit over to some bushes before someone spotted him lying there. She got out and walked around to the front of the car afraid at first to even look at the body. But knowing she had little or no time to waste she moved in grabbing the body by the shoulders and half-lifting, half-dragging the lifeless form to the waiting secrecy of the brushes.

Jamie returned to her car and retrieving a towel from the back seat went around to the hood and tried her best to wipe the blood from the shiny silver metallic surface of her rented Mercury Sable. She then got into the car and moved it closer to the ramp where the delivery trucks back up to unload their goods, getting as close to the door as possible so Zach would not have far to go when he exited the building.

Jamie put the car into park and started to turn off the engine but stopped and decided to leave it running thinking that Zach should be coming out any moment. "But what if he doesn't? What if he's hurt or gets caught?" she thinks, that worried feeling suddenly creeping back into her mind again. "No time to get hysterical," she says, as she tries to shake off the dreadful feeling.

*   *   *

Zach decided it was time to call Rusty into the room and work or not, the plan was as good as it was going to get. "If this works and I see Jamie again, I'm never setting foot in another lab as long as I live," Zach promised to himself.

Zach went to the door and knocked on it to draw the attention of the guard. Rusty, who was half dosing, jumped with a start and got up out of his chair.

Rusty was aware that Morganthau and Whiteslayer intended to do away with the scientist named Zach as soon as he had completed what ever it is they had locked him in the room to do. Rusty always thought of himself as a passive kind of guy. He wasn't in to violence for the fun of it and that is just how Morganthau and Whiteslayer came off to him. That is why should anything go down and he could help the guy in some way to escape then he would do it. He did not know what just yet but he would think of something.

Zach stepped back away from the door to let Rusty enter the room and his heart dropped when he saw Rusty close the door behind him as he entered. Zach knew the only way he could get out would be to unlock the door and the keys were hanging off of Rusty's belt. "That's it," he thought. "There is no way I am going to get out of here alive," Zach thought dejectedly.

"So what's up doc," Rusty said with a smile.

"I need you to help me finish this experiment and I can not do it by myself with my wrist broken and all," Zach managed.

"No problem man. Just show me what you need done."

Rusty decided when he entered the room he would just come right out and say something to Zach and see if they could come up with a plan.

"Look Zach, I know you're in a lot of trouble here and all and I know is that Morganthau has no intention of letting you go when you're done doing whatever it is you do here. I think it would be a good idea if we could stage an accident and get you out of here."

Zach was floored. He was too shocked to reply at first but then recovered enough to say, "thanks Rusty, you do not know how I have hoped something like this would happen."

"I knew as soon as I told Morganthau the job was finished he would turn Whiteslayer loose on me and I'd wind up being fish food in a nearby lake somewhere."

"I have no doubt you're right about that, Zach. That is why I've been sitting outside that door for the last eight hours trying to come up with a plan to get you out of here."

"Rusty, a plan is already in progress. My girlfriend is, as we speak, trying to create a diversion while I find a way past you and to the bay doors outside."

"Well, if someone was to hit me in the head with that stool over there I could pretend to be knocked out long enough for you to get the keys and let yourself out of the lab."

"I'm not sure if I can do that," Zach said.

"It's your only chance Zach."

"I'll be fine and when they come to get you they will find me unconscious and laying on the floor. They will just think you hit me and escaped."

Before Rusty could speak the alarms in the main building started to go off. They both looked at each other for a second before saying anything.

"Sounds like your plan is working so you better get to it."

Zach grabbed the stool and with as much force has he dared he swung the stool and hit Rusty just behind the back of the head. The stool connected with the back of Rusty's head with a dull thud and Rusty was sent sprawling forward on to the counter and then fell to the floor with a crash.

"Are you all right Rusty?" Zach asked seeing blood flow from a gash on the back of Rusty's head.

"Yeah, now get before Whiteslayer comes and does us both in," Rusty said as he reached to staunch the flow of blood.

"Move it now Zach."

Zach dropped the stool and grabbed the keys from Rusty's belt and ran for the door. He had trouble finding the right key at first but then got the door unlocked and was running down the hall to the exit. As Zach reached the door and began to open it the main door at the other end of the lab flew open and Whiteslayer stepped through.

"Zach, Freeze!" Whiteslayer yelled.

Zach stopped and turned raising his hands in the air.

"I'm a goner for sure now," Zach thought as he watched Whiteslayer advance toward him with his pistol drawn.

With a sneer etched across his otherwise stoic face, Whiteslayer advanced down the hall toward where Zach stood. Zach momentarily thought of trying to make a last ditch effort to escape as he held the exit door to the lab half-open, and only a few feet from where Jamie waited in her car but the look in Whiteslayer's eyes convinced him the attempt would be in vain.

"Zach walk slowly back into the building and close the door now."

"And if I don't?" Zach asked trying to delay the inevitable.

"Then I'll kill you where you stand," said Whiteslayer.

Whiteslayer lowered his pistol until it was aimed at Zach's heart and pulled back the hammer of the Glock pistol. He started to squeeze the trigger when a single shot to the back of the chest hit him. The impact caused Whiteslayer to pitch forward and land at Zach's feet where he stood by the door.

Zach was momentarily shocked at the turn of events. Just then Rusty came from around the corner where he had been crouching and stood and looked at Zach.

"Go on, get out of here. I'll clean up this mess myself," Rusty said.

"Thanks, Rusty. You saved my ass again. I won't forget it," Zach said.

"Go on, get," Rusty waved.

Zach turned and ran out the door and stopped when he saw Jamie standing by the car.

"Jamie!" he yelled.

"What happened?" Jamie asked as they both ran to each other and embraced and kissed.

Zach ran his hands through Jamie's hair and said, "What happened to that beautiful blonde I admired so much?"

"No time for that now. Let's get out of here while we still can," Jamie replied.

Jamie and Zach ran for the car and jumped in but before he could put the car in gear Jamie looked at him and said, "after all we've been through don't you think it would be wise to put on your seat belt?"

"Yes Ma'am!" he said and threw her a salute.

He tossed the car into gear and spun the tires as he headed for the street. As they sped away Zach touched the pocket of his shirt and realized with a smile that he still had his Technadine security clearance badge in his shirt pocket. He pulled it out and turned it over in his hands and with a smile flicked it out the car window where it landed at the feet of a fireman who was responding to the fire in the main building. Zach and Jamie looked back at the building and all the people standing around outside and then turned to each other and smiled.

Jamie said, "Well Mister Denton, just what are your intentions?"

"To be with the girl of my dreams," Zach said as he smiled and clasped his hand in hers.

Zach turned onto Hwy 101 and headed for the airport.

"Don't you want to stop and pick up some of your things from your apartment?" Jamie asked.

"No, I have everything I need right here," Zach said with a smile.

Chapter 27

March 15, 2001
2:00 p.m.
Isle of St. Martin

On a sunny afternoon eight months later, Zach, sporting a full beard and much longer hair, lounged under a huge umbrella with a large pink flamingo painted on it. Sipping a Piña Colada he watched languidly as the tourist's wandered up and down the beach collecting sea shells and generally going about their vacations on this popular Caribbean isle. Zach looked over at Jamie, who sensing that she is being stared at, glances up from the latest book she is reading called "Running With The Tide" by a promising new author the cover jacket proclaims, as Zach says, "it's time."

He reaches for the phone and begins to dial the list of numbers on the sheet of paper that lies crumpled in his lap. He doesn't have to look at them as he dials each one for he has memorized every one of them by heart. He had secretly hacked into Technadine's main computer several months earlier and had managed to retrieve the names, addresses and phone numbers of every person who had been implanted with the chips. He had patiently waited for the right moment to access the files at Technadine's headquarters so that he would only have to break into the system once and then get out before anyone detected that he had been there.

Then, he had waited. Reading the newspapers for world events, watching the news for approaching elections in various countries around the world and important meetings with the U.S. government and key governments around the globe. Zach had listened with interest this morning as the news station on this small tropic isle had issued a statement that the head of Technadine Corporation had been in talks with several governments on the arms treaty being discussed in the Middle East.

Zach knew it was time. Time to shut down Morganthau's operation and cut the man himself down before he could do the world great harm.

Chapter 28

March 15, 2001
2:00 p.m.
Silicon Valley, California

Douglas has just come from a high-level meeting with top officials in the US Government and heads-of-state from several Middle Eastern countries.

"They left with less balls than they came in with that's for sure," Douglas thought smiling to himself as he pulled into his personal parking space at Technadine's headquarters.

He was turning the screws on the US officials to heat up the Middle East involvement. Morganthau had manipulated the government from the very beginning on Operation Echo. He secretly had Zach make extra chips and had them implanted into his own operatives. Because of his close association with world governments through his company's business dealings Morganthau was able to introduce his operatives into those governments he ultimately wished to control.

Morganthau now had operatives in place in four third world countries and two world powers. He was now able to control those governments by eavesdropping on their top officials and then using their own information against them. Technadine's presence had more than doubled in those countries where his operatives worked and Douglas found himself in the enviable position of hosting dinners to Prime Ministers and Dictators alike.

In just six months his company had more than doubled in size and revenues. Morganthau himself was now considered the richest man in the world having easily surpassed the Bill Gates' and Donald Trump's of the world. He could do and say whatever he wanted and they would break backs to kiss his ass.

"Life was good," Douglas thought.

Just then his cell phone rang and he reached to retrieve it from its cradle on the console of his car.

"This is Morganthau," he said.

"Hello Douglas," Zach said.

"Zach? Is that you?" Morganthau replied. "Where are you, you sniveling little shit,"

"Somewhere where you can not reach me," Zach replied.

"You can not hide Zach. You know it is only a matter of time before we find you."

"Why do you want to kill me? You got what you wanted. The chips are finished and you have no doubt used them for your little scheme already. So why am I still on your little hit list?" Zach said.

"Because Zach, I can not have you running around trying to spoil all I have worked for. All I have tried to achieve. You're the only one who knows anything about my plans," Morganthau fumed.

"It's nothing personal Zach, but you understand, I can not have you spoiling my little secret."

"Well it's too bad your plan is not going to work, Douglas. You're never going to get to use the technology for your own good. You're never going to enjoy the fruits of your labor," Zach said.

"Oh, but I have already, Zach. The chips are indeed in place and as we speak my operatives are stationed all over the globe doing my bidding. So you see Zach, there is nothing you can do to stop me now, and as soon as I find you it well no longer be your problem."

Zach was tiring of talking to Morganthau. It sickened him to think this man had gotten away with so much all ready. That one man could cause so much pain and suffering all in the name of power.

Zach Denton had waited six long months to say just three simple words. Three insignificant words he had secretly programmed into every chip that he had created for Technadine Corporation those many months ago. When Zach phoned each person on the list he now held in his hand and spoke those three tiny words the processor he had put his whole being into, his lifelong dream, would melt under extreme heat and fuse all living tissue and blood vessels around it. It would be a painful but swift death.

"All too swift," Zach thought as he turned his attention back to Morganthau.

"It's just a matter of time before my men find you and that bitch friend of yours," Morganthau screamed. "I have the power to go any-where, anytime and no one can stop me. I have the ultimate power."

"Power isn't everything," Zach said as he hung up the phone.

With those three little words spoken, a self-destruct message was sent to the chip implanted in Morganthau's brain.

Suddenly Morganthau was racked with pain by a throbbing, ringing-like sound in his head. Douglas clenched the steering wheel of his '42 Bentley. The pain had become white hot and seemed to emanate from the chip that was planted inside his head. A searing heat seemed to grow inside his head and he suddenly realized what Zach had done. As the pain began to overcome him and he started to slip forward onto the steering wheel of his prized automobile, Morganthau realized that Zach had outsmarted him. Zach had cheated him out of possibly becoming one of the most powerful people in the whole world. This sorry little man had won and had taken him, Douglas J. Morganthau down.

Chapter 29

March 15, 2001
2:30 p.m. (Pacific Time)

International Newswire Service—dated 03/15/2001—2:30 p.m. Pacific Standard Time

Reports are still coming in all over the world as we speak. Seven prominent leaders and at least two heads of state from nine countries have all been found dead today. Initial reports indicate that they all died from massive brain hemorrhages within minutes apart from each other. Investigations into a possible terrorist link have already begun and an emergency session of the United Nations has been called.

In an unrelated case the President of one of the most powerful corporations in the world has died today of a stroke. A spokesman for the company, Technadine Corporation, has issued a statement that Douglas J. Morganthau passed away this afternoon at approximately 2:00 p.m. Pacific Standard Time, while sitting in his car just outside the companies headquarters in Silicon Valley.

About the Author

Samuel J. Zewe was born in Brownsville, Texas in 1958. He currently resides in Houston, Texas with his wife, Barbara and their three dogs. He divides his time between his two loves, writing and painting.

www.ingramcontent.com/pod-product-compliance
Lightning Source LLC
LaVergne TN
LVHW041102090125
800888LV00006B/89